"Try minding your own beeswax, Raider. Just once in your life."

"You *are* my beeswax, Doc. We're still a team, till this thing's wrapped up an' in the journal. So don' go lettin' yourself get too distracted."

Doc grinned. "You know something? I believe you're jealous! You are, aren't you?"

"Oh, hell yes. Green with envy, that's me. I mean whores are 'bout as scarce 'round these parts as a bull in a belfry."

"Don't start..."

"Oh, go screw yourself. On second thought, don't. No need to go makin' her nibs jealous."

With this Raider walked away, and Doc stood seething.

J. D. HARDIN

TOMBSTONE IN DEADWOOD

Ⓑ®

BERKLEY BOOKS, NEW YORK

TOMBSTONE IN DEADWOOD

A Berkley Book / published by arrangement with
the author

PRINTING HISTORY
Berkley edition / November 1984

ISBN: 0-425-07461-7

A BERKLEY BOOK ® TM 757,375
Berkley Books are published by Berkley Publishing Group,
200 Madison Avenue, New York, N.Y. 10016.
The name "BERKLEY" and the stylized "B" with design
are trademarks belonging to Berkley Publishing Corporation.

PRINTED IN THE UNITED STATES OF AMERICA

CHAPTER ONE

Raider had little fondness for Dakota Territory, and considerably less for Deadwood, his destination. He had visited the overblown mining camp spawned in the gold rush of '75 on four separate occasions previously. Twelve months after the first tents and false fronts had been hurriedly thrown up, the population was close to twenty-five thousand, and the number of saloons, sporting houses, parlor houses, cribs, and various other hostels of iniquity had increased accordingly. Lowlifes generally bring their evil and their iron with them when descending upon a locale, and the streets of Deadwood rang with gunfire around the clock. Along with intended targets, stray lead found many an innocent, and funerals were discouragingly frequent.

Dying by accident had to be the sorriest of ways to go, he had very early decided. After all the scrapes and hazards to hide he had lived through over the past fifteen years, to cash his chips in courtesy of some drunk's unaimed bullet in the back was a prospect both upsetting and worrisome. His plan was clear and easy of execution, at least in mind: get into town, join Doc, together arrest Sam Bass and Joel Collins, and ride out as fast as horse legs could carry them.

Leaning forward, he ruffled the little grulla mustang's mane and patted her neck affectionately. She had brought him all the way from Great Bend, Kansas, better than 450 miles, where he had been tarrying, courtesy of a grievously painful gunshot wound in the shoulder, his by virtue of a particularly witless imbroglio involving three would-be bank robbers. He and his partner, Doc Weatherbee, had made short work of same, saving the Great Bend Farmers & Merchants Bank's assets on hand, the employees' hides, and preserving their own hitherto all but unblemished reputations as first-rate Pinkerton operatives. Now he had only his rapidly healing wound to remind him of the incident, and remind him it did every time he lifted his arm too quickly or rolled over onto it in bed.

Why, he mused, do people who, if their lives depended on it, couldn't hit the side of a barn from the inside, take up guns and careers as high line riders?

"Assholes!"

He had been following meandering Elk Creek westward into a sun that resembled a ladleful of molten copper pouring as neatly across the horizon as flapjack batter onto a grill. Beneath it the dark green pines robing the hills lent them a brooding aspect at this distance, providing them with their name. Deadwood lay about twenty miles ahead. To the north, beyond a low-lying ridge, Alkali Creek ran parallel to Elk, almost but not quite into the Fort Meade military reservation east of Deadwood on a line. They wouldn't be needing the Army's help in this go-round, he reflected, but it was comforting to know Mr. Blue was in the neighborhood, just in case.

Gingerly, he flexed his shoulder. So dull was the pain it was barely noticeable. It itched, though, which, although annoying, was a good sign. At least he had come through it without infection setting in, no thanks to the foul-breathed and filthy-fingered self-styled doctor who had dug out the shot and washed the hole clean with whiskey, setting his hair on end and liberating a scream loud enough to wake the dead, punctuated by a torrent of cursing.

He had refused to pay the four-dollar fee demanded by the butchering bastard, claiming he wasn't fit to treat a suck-egg mule, let alone humans in hurt. A loud and spirited argument had followed, and he had tossed two greenbacks at him and stalked out, bearing with him equivalent burdens of pain and anger.

The sun now lay like an egg yolk on the crest of the hills ahead. The shadows lengthened and merged into a dark, velvety carpet. The grass bowed to a passing breeze, and he thought about his partner, Doc. He missed old Wise-mouth, Mr. College-Education-Ladies-Man-Flasharity with his curly-brim derby, outrageously expensive custom-tailored broadcloth suit, black and gold checkered faro dealer's vest, and imported Italian soft leather shoes.

"About as useful for riding up and down the territories as a boil on a bride's ass, damn fool!"

Damned fool though Doc may have been, he did miss him. Three weeks was a long time for partners to be sep-arated. Much can happen. He hoped he was okay, not in dutch, not hurt or ailing, sober and not broke. If he was broke he'd be damned if he'd lend him anything.

"Not a penny! If you don't know how to handle your money that's your problem. Don't come round chiselin' my hard-earned pay." He winced slightly as his wound re-asserted its presence. "Hard-earned's right. You're out o' luck, Weatherbee!"

He continued to berate Doc for his spendthrift ways for the next few miles, the grulla flicking its ears in agreement. It was dark by the time they came within sight of Deadwood. Yellow lights pricked the moonless night like fireflies frozen in flight. Almost before he saw the town, he could hear it, gunfire at that distance thumping like a great ceremonial drum being tested. Deadwood sat on hilly ground in the canyon of Whitewood Creek at an elevation of more than three-quarters of a mile, surrounded by well-worked but still productive gold mines, including the far-famed Homestake. The available ore was low grade, Raider knew, yielding from two to eight dollars a ton, but it was vast in quantity, easily mined, and the gold extracted by the simple process of stamping and amalgamation.

He stiffened, reining the grulla to slow her pace. Disgust welled in his chest. He hated the idea of riding in. The sporadic but no less lethal gunfire was becoming louder, sharper. The timber-covered slopes prevented the town from

4   J. D. HARDIN

growing laterally, so that it had to be built along a single
narrow main street. Coming to the head of it, a quarter mile
distant, it beckoned almost threateningly.

"Come on in and bring your blood."

In its earlier years Deadwood had hosted such notable
characters as Calamity Jane, Poker Alice Ivers, Wild Bill
Hickok, Wyatt Earp, Doc Holliday, and a small yard full
of Deadwood Dicks. Raider closed his eyes and saw once
more the Bucket of Blood, Montana, and Nutthall and Mann's
No. 10 Saloon, where Hickok was shot dead while playing
cards. Visiting entertainers performed at the Gem and Bella
Union theaters. Gamblers pressed their luck at the Green
Front Sporting House, Sam Bass and Joel Collins's combination brothel and gambling casino, and other establish-
ments devoted to shearing lambs and lions alike. He had
been unable to give Doc any idea as to when he would arrive
in town. "In two or three weeks" had been his last words
at their parting in Great Bend, after receiving the telegram
from Wagner in Chicago, ordering them to head for Deadwood.

He planted the heel of his hand on his holstered .45, his
eyes narrowing and darting left and right as he rode into
town. It hadn't changed, he thought. On second thought it
had: It was even louder, courser, wilder, more disgusting,
more ridiculous than on his last visit. Two men came flying
through the batwing doors of Montana, tossed out by twin
bald-headed, bull-headed, barrel-bellied booming bartenders in identical filthy aprons. One of the bum-rushed ones
rolled over, forcing his face into the mud, the other struggled
to his knees and fell sideways, his head smashing against
the end of the horse trough, slumping him into a motionless
heap. Raider clucked disapprovingly. The noise was fear-
some; it poured from the saloons, gambling houses, and
dance halls, slamming against his eardrums. How anybody
could sleep through it was a mystery to him.

Reaching the center of town, he pulled left, dismounted,
hitched the grulla, and set about looking for Doc.

But it was Doc who found Raider, spotting him and
calling out, "Rade!"

Doc was standing against the corner of the Green Front Sporting House. Raider's brows knit in puzzlement at first sight of him. His derby was tilted uncharacteristically backward on his head, his vest was unfastened, his clothing disheveled. Balancing on one leg, his back supported by the building, he held his other leg across his knee and appeared to be scraping mud from the shoe in his hand. He finished the task to his satisfaction and was putting the shoe back on when Raider came up to him. Immediately, he began straightening his clothing.

"You look a damned wreck, you know that?" began Raider amiably.

"Look who's talking," replied Doc. "When's the last time you had a bath? Don't you own a razor? Your breath smells like you've been chewing on a hog wallow. You're filthy as a Turk."

"It's a pleasure seein' you, too. Don' go tryin' to cover up your own self." Raider's voice softened. "Something wrong?"

"Not a blessed thing." Doc, too, softened his tone. "How's your shoulder?"

"All knit and itchin' to beat the band. What's with our friends, Mr. Fish and his sidekick?"

"If you mean Sam Bass and Joel Collins, they're out of town."

"Jesus Christ!"

"Take it easy, they're coming back."

A gambling man and a whore came sailing by, all giggles, bringing on the mingled stenches of cheap perfume and cheaper stogie smoke. Raider stared at them sourly. The gambler's fox face darkened in a scowl.

"Something troubling you, brother?"

"Hell no, 'brother.' I take it you and your sister there are on your way to church. Would you mind puttin' a dime in the God box for me?"

"Rade..." began Doc wearily.

"What does he mean by that? Waz he mean!" shrilled the lady, flouncing and bristling indignantly, her dark eyes stabbing Raider.

"Nothing, nothing," blurted Doc, grabbing Raider by the elbow and shoving him down the sidewalk.

"Goddamn dumb-ass whore. Stupid tinhorn."

"Will you put a plug in it, for heaven's sakes? You're not in town two minutes and already you're looking for trouble."

"Can't stand lowlifes."

"Bass and Collins are coming back. They'll be here in a few days. We shouldn't have any difficulty taking them. We've got surprise on our side; all we have to do is get the drop on them. Our orders are to escort them down to Big Spring, Texas, and turn them over to the Howard County sheriff."

"What about the U.P. payroll they stole? Close to eighty thousand, as I recall."

"We'll get it, what they haven't spent of it. Speaking of money . . ." Doc stopped, stopping Raider short. "As luck would have it, I suddenly find myself a little short."

"What are you talkin' about, 'luck'? You been playing stud with strangers? Three-card monte?"

"No, no, no." Doc waved away both suggestions with manifest indignation. "Nothing of the kind. What on earth do you take me for?"

"The answer to that don' answer the question."

He stood staring at his partner. Doc's confidence seemed to seep slowly from him. His smile vanished, his handsome face sagging into a sheepish expression, bringing his shoulders and his entire upper body down with it. His eyes were firmly fastened on the tips of his shoes as he explained. While awaiting Raider's arrival he had been frequenting the Green Front Sporting House, at first merely kibitizing the play, then becoming attracted to a marathon dice game, studying the participants, assessing their intelligence and their luck, deciding at length that he could take them, joining the game, promptly dropping $94, leaving him with $8 and change, dropping out, coming back the next night, winning $62, coming back a third time, winning $118, coming back a fourth time . . .

"Losing it all," rasped Raider irritably.

"Not all." Doc held up a greasy-looking quarter.

"You're funny as hell, you know that? Don' you know by now, you with all your high-priced schoolin' an' college an' readin' an' junk, that dice in Deadwood has got to be as fixed as a shoe on a horse? Loaded, shaved, rigged one way or the other, sittin' on the felt just waitin' for some bean-brained asshole like you to come saunterin' in with a fresh green roll just achin' to be taken? Don' you know that by now? Don' you know nothin'? Can't you learn nothin'? Can't I teach you? Goddamn Sam an' Bertha if you're not the limit!"

"Easy, Rade, keep it down. I'm in no mood for a lecture. Have a heart! A man of intelligence, culture, and breeding like myself could go stark, staring mad in a sinkhole like this. I . . . I did it to preserve my sanity! As the good Lord is my witness."

"If he is an' hears you lyin' like that he's liable to strike you dead in those fancy-ass shoes you're standin' in!"

"Be a sport, payday's three days from now. You know Wagner; we may not get much, but we do get it on time. Lend me fifty and I swear by all that's sacred you'll get it back as soon as we're paid. With interest."

The last two words discernibly softened the glower that had taken possession of Raider's well-stubbled face.

"How much?"

"How about five percent?"

"How about twenty-five."

"Ten." Doc shoved his hand into his partner's. "Deal?"

Raider reached for his heart pocket, bringing out his money. "Only got 'bout eighty bucks." He paused, his eyes slitting. "What you plannin' to do, go back into that shithole an' lose *it,* too?"

"No, no, no. It's for the hotel."

"How come? You don' pay till you check out."

"It's not for me." He held forth his hand. "Give it here."

Slowly, reluctantly, Raider counted out four crumpled tens and two even more crumpled fives. The bills disappeared into Doc's lower vest pocket so quickly his hand became a blur.

"What do you mean, 'not for me'?"

"Let me be honest with you."

"That's a switch."

"I've ... I've met a girl, a lady. Her name is Lydia-Mae Breed. Blond, blue-eyed, lovely, just beautiful. Wait'll you meet her!"

Raider eyed him in shocked disbelief. "You serious?"

"I've never been more so. She's the light of my life. For the first time in my life I'm really and truly in love."

"You're really an' truly nuts!"

"Thanks to Lydia I'm a changed man. Brace yourself. We're going to be married."

"Shit and two are eight."

"In ten days, right here in Deadwood. In the Methodist Church. Then ... brace yourself again. I'm retiring."

"Oh, balls!"

"Absolutely. This business with Bass and Collins and the U.P. payroll is my last assignment. I haven't notified Chicago yet, and won't till after we've wound things up. I've made an ironclad promise to Lydia. The Pinkerton National Detective Agency and I are quits. Permanently. My brilliant career as a crime fighter is over. We're heading back east, I'll enroll in a prestigious law school, probably Harvard. Failing Harvard, Yale will have to do. I'll earn my degree, pass the bar, and establish myself in the profession, probably in Boston. I love Boston. Lydia will too. I'll work like the proverbial Trojan, become rich and famous, and she and I will live happily ever after."

"Got it figured out to a tee, ain'cha?"

"Don't try and talk me out of it. You'll just be wasting your breath. My mind's made up. You know it had to come to this sooner or later. It's been fun, it's been fascinating, knowing you, working with you shoulder to shoulder. It's been, for the most part, a positive joy."

"Shut it off, will you? You're gettin' the whole entire street knee deep in horseshit."

"I'm deadly serious, Rade. Talk is cheap. You need to be convinced. I'll introduce you two."

"I can't wait to meet her. Look at me, I'm all prickly

pins and needles. We better get a move on afore I bust out in sweat and shakin'."

Doc patted his newly acquired roll in his vest pocket. "She's staying at the Deadwood Hotel. The manager asked me to put a little something down on her bill. Gesture of good faith."

"He afraid she'll snooker him out of it? What is she, some kinda flimflam artist?"

Doc bristled briefly, then grinned. "Let's go. I'm dying to introduce you."

"I'm dyin' to meet her."

"That's my boy."

"This should be good for sixteen laughs."

Lydia-Mae Breed *was* as pretty, as fetching as Doc had painted her in Raider's imagination. Dressed in a flouncy taffeta dress spattered with tiny pink rosebuds, with a black velvet ribbon around her slender neck, an ivory brooch at her throat, and a delicate spray of flowers in her lovely blond hair, she looked every inch a lady. To the untutored eye.

Unfortunately for Doc, Raider's eye was tutored. In the doorway he returned her smile with a speedily mustered but undeniably false one of his own, shook her outstretched hand, and effectively stifled a groan. The new light of Doc's life, the delight of his dreams, the fair fascinator of his future was a whore. Raider had seen enough whores in his day to be able to spot one at fifty paces, regardless of garb, degree of delicate affectation, beauty, freedom from soil and decay, and makeup. In his solidly dependable experience whores had, without exception, a certain aura about them, an ever-so-slight falsity in their smile, a come-hither-with-a-dollar gleam in their eye, a swing to their hips— force of habit—that sounded a silent alarm. Operative Weatherbee had corraled himself a working girl. Raider's eyes slid sideways at his partner beside him as Doc started forward. Lydia-Mae stood aside, her hand on the door.

He had to know, reflected Raider dourly. In some ways he was green as new grass. In the enticing proximity of

tumbling dice, for example. But he wasn't stupid. He knew
the difference between good goods and soiled, the difference
between a hooker and a choir singer on sight as well as he.

Introductions and idle chitchat followed. Raider sat on
the end of the neatly made bed, slowly revolving his hat in
his hands, all but deaf to the conversation, his mind whirl-
ing. *If* Doc knew, and he had to know, what was the idea,
the attraction? Converting her? Ringing her finger and thereby
washing away the past? Setting her dainty feet on the path
of righteousness strewn with the roses of respectability?
Such a challenge would be attractive to him. Just his dish
of tea.

Mrs. Weatherbee-to-be spoke.

"Doc's told me so much about you I feel as if we're
already old friends."

"Yeah."

"You must forgive Raider's appearance, my dearest. He's
come a long way."

A small knot of nausea rolled over in Raider's gut as
Doc's hand seized hers, squeezing it, and following this up
with a loving peck to the cheek.

"It's such a pleasure meeting you at last," gushed Lydia-
Mae. "This calls for a celebration."

"It does indeed. Rade, what do you say you and I hop
down to the nearest saloon and pick up a bottle of cham-
pagne?"

With my money, of course, mused Raider. Doc was on
his feet, retrieving his hat from the night table.

"We won't be long, darling."

Raider groaned inwardly. None of this was happening.
It was all a bad dream, a nightmare experienced while ver-
tical and wide awake. Was that possible? Moments later he
was following Doc back down the stairs to the lobby.

"Doc..."

"I know, I know, she's a working girl. So? Does that
make her a criminal? Is she condemned to hell for all eter-
nity?"

"Doc..."

"Actually, that's the whole point, friend. She's not. Not

anymore. We've agreed to renounce our . . . former lives."

"Beautiful. Can I ask you a honest question? Ever hear the story about the polecat that met the handsome prince an' overnight turned into one o' them bird-o'-paradises?"

Doc, preceding him, had reached the lobby. He stopped short and turned very slowly.

"You want to start something, Rade, I'll finish it."

"I'm not knockin' the lady. I'm only talkin' 'bout the impossibilities o' life, the things that just can't never can be. Birds that swim, fish that fly. Jesus Christ, I'm only thinkin' o' you."

"Oh? Are you sure losing your partner isn't worrying you just a trifle? Frankly, I'm sorry about that part of it. I . . . I feel a little like a deserter."

"You goddamn should!"

No one was occupying any of the cheap, battered, overstuffed chairs in the lobby, although former, recent occupants had left a pall of blue-gray smoke hanging in the fetid air. The sight of it prompted Doc to action. Extracting an Old Virginia cheroot from a shiny new brass case, he lit up. He proudly displayed the case for Raider's benefit.

"Little gift from Lydia-Mae. Initialed and everything."

"Mmmmm."

"Rade, Rade, Rade." He sighed in mingled frustration and exasperation. "I realize all this comes as a big shock to you, but that's the way it is. I didn't plan it this way. It's my life, and I'll do as I please with it. I'm sorry if you're disappointed."

"Disgusted is more like it. Revolted."

Doc shrugged. "Whatever. What do you say we drop it? Make it off-limits as a subject for conversation. We'll only go round and round like two dogs yapping at their tails and end up at each other's throats."

He paused. Raider's glance had deserted him, drawn to the front desk and the soft, moist, rhythmical snoring of the clerk, his head down on his forearms, his bald pate reflecting the overhead lamp. Doc's observation prompted a thought. About ending discussion of it he was right, but apart from that, he, Raider, was damned and doomed if he'd stand idly

by and let the bastard blithely toss his life away on some
no-good piece of dollar ass. Not a chance, Weatherbee. If
you won't listen to reason, I'll just have to try another
approach. Like it or lump it, no goddamn partner o' this
old boy is going to make a damn fool of himself, ruin a
perfectly good career, wreck his future, and leave me with
a worm in my conscience. Damn me for a cross-eyed jackass
if I keep my nose out of this one and wake up ten years
from now up to my eyeballs in regret, wishing I went and
took the bull by the horns when I should ought to have!

"If you think I'm gonna live the rest o' my life with you
on my conscience," he muttered, "you got another think
comin'."

"What was that?"

"Nothin'."

"Nothing positive or encouraging, from the look on your
face."

"All right, all right, all right. I'm not gonna knock her
or you. You want to get hitched, go ahead."

"That's better. As if you meant it."

"I do, I do."

Raider was as good as his word in the hours that followed.
He kept his opinion of Lydia-Mae to himself, along with
his views of his partner's intelligence, judgment, even sanity. The following afternoon the two of them stood across
the street from Bass and Collins's brothel—gambling house,
casually casing the place while Lydia-Mae enjoyed her
"beauty sleep." Doc's mention of this to Raider as they
departed the hotel tempted the plowboy to comment that
she might better spend the time taking a bath and washing
away the first coating of sin, but he discreetly held his piece.

"You been inside yet?" Raider asked, nodding toward
the two-story frame building. It had been freshly painted
white, and fairly sparkled in the bright sunlight.

A surrey with what Raider would observe was a decent,
respectable, God-fearing and hay-avoiding young lady at
the reins trundled by. Doc sighed softly, following her with

his eyes. All such adjectives may well have described her; unfortunately, she had a shape vaguely suggesting a bull fiddle and a face that would stop a rampaging ox. When only the blind look at you on the street, it must be easy to be pure, he reflected.

"Once."

"Just to check it out, right?"

"In a way. Actually...ahem...well, it happens that's where I met Lydia."

Raider gasped theatrically. "She..."

Doc nodded. "Had to work someplace," he snapped stiffly.

"So she knows Mr. Fish and his friend."

"Not intimately." It was a poor choice of words, prompting a suggestive leer on Raider's part. "I told you before, they'll be back in a day or so. Our best bet will be to try and catch them together outside. We'll have to be careful. They're sure to have a load of friends in this town."

"Did she tell you that?"

"Isn't it logical? With a little luck maybe we can front and back them on the sidewalk, get them into the nearest alley, one of us covers them, the other gets our horses, and we all take off for Texas."

"What about her?"

"We've already discussed it. She knows I have to complete the assignment. She accepts it."

"We could easily wind it up before you two get hitched."

"If we do, we'll simply postpone the wedding." Doc smiled slyly. "Unless, of course, you'd be willing to take Bass and Collins down to Big Spring by yourself. Do you think you could handle the two of them?"

"Oh, hell no!"

"We could consider it your wedding present to us."

"Hell, I can do lots better than that. Buy you a family Bible, one o' them big heavy ones with the gilt trim an' a blue ribbon for marking the last verse you read. Or how's about a nice carpet sweeper? Maybe a carpet. How about some soup bowls?"

"You're funny, Rade. Seriously, in the event Bass and

Collins do turn up before the wedding, we'll take them in and Lydia and I'll meet somewhere between here and Big Spring. I'd like you to be my best man, Rade."

"I'll most likely be the only man. This part o' the country isn' exactly crawlin' with friends o' yours. Course, she must know a lot o' fellas." Doc stiffened. "Only funnin'."

"About Bass and Collins. Collins is easygoing, good with a gun, but not a hothead. Not likely to put up a fight when we move in. Bass is another story."

"You don' have to tell me 'bout that son of a bitch. Him I know by rep from way back. Can't read or write. Started out racin' horses an' gamblin', took to rustlin', cleaned up proper, cut some bloody path through Texas, the U.P. job, an' wound up here. You know, while we're standin' here jawin' they could be off blowin' a bank or a Wells Fargo office. How come when you showed up an' found they'd lit out you didn' go after 'em?"

"Had to wait for my slow-bones partner. Chief's orders. We're a team, remember?"

"I remember. You seem to be the one with the memory trouble."

Doc let the dig pass without comment and moments later excused himself to go and get his hair cut.

"You could use one yourself, Rade."

"I could use the twenty-five cents better."

"You look like a drowned dog. When are you going to shave?"

"What's it to you?"

"I hope before the wedding."

Doc waved and walked off. Raider let him get out of sight around the corner of the livery stable where he was boarding his horse, then took off at a trot in the direction of the Deadwood Hotel. Hurrying up the front steps, he paused at the twin glass doors, eyeing his image, finger-combing his hair, smoothing his eyebrows and mustache with spit.

"Han'some fuckin' devil, you!"

In he barged, nearly upsetting an elderly dowager who shrank to one side and eyed him in vicious disapproval.

Ignoring her, he crossed the lobby and bounded up the stairs. Locating room number 2C, he preened himself hastily one last time, removed his hat, took a deep breath, and knocked.

"Who is it?"

"Me, Raider. Sorry if I woke you."

The door opened. She was dressed in a fetching bright red dress with dainty lace collar and cuffs.

"You didn't. Come in."

He closed the door behind him. "Goodness, don' you look pretty as a damn swan. Red sure enough's your color."

"Thank you. Where's Doc?"

"Went to get a haircut."

"What did you want?"

"Nothin'. Not really." He stared at her. "Jus' come up to say hello."

There followed an awkward pause. She went to the wash-basin and began fussing with her hair in the large oval mirror.

"Raider?"

"Yeah?"

"You don't approve of me, do you?"

"What are you talkin' 'bout?"

She whirled on him, her pretty face annoyed, accusing. "You think I'm just another whore who's gotten her hooks into your best friend."

"I never said that."

"You don't have to, it's written all over your face every time you look at me. Let me tell you something, mister. It just might help you understand. He loves me and I love him. It's that simple. Perhaps I have done a few things in my life to be ashamed of, I'm not denying that, but it's all over now. He's giving me a fresh start, and I intend to make the most of it. I'm going to be a good wife to him. The best."

Raider nodded slowly and, gliding to the door, his hands behind his back, locked it.

"What do you think you're doing?" she asked tightly.

"I rather we didn' have nobody interruptin' us."

"Unlock it."

"No, please, bear with me. I'm not gonna hurt you or nothin'."

"I didn't think you would."

She sat at the foot of the bed. He approached her. "You're a very pretty woman, Lydia. It's sure not hard to see how come he fell for you. You're downright beautiful."

"Raider, maybe you'd better say what you came to say, then leave. I'm beginning to feel uncomfortable."

"I'm sorry. You are beautiful." He dug in his pocket and brought out a dollar, tossing it on the bed. She shot to her feet, her eyes widening.

"What the devil . . ."

"Oh, c'mon. Don' go gettin' all huffy."

"Are you out of your mind?"

"Do I got to spell it out for you?"

"You already have, you bastard!"

"Hey, hey, hey." Out came another dollar, landing beside the first.

She gasped. Picking up both, she flung them at him. "Get out!"

"Oh, for Chrissakes! You tryin' to tell me you won' lay down for two whole dollars cash money? Hell, that's twice what any other whore in all the territories gets. Double, missy. So what do you say, let's get to rompin'. Nothin' fancy. Me, I go the simple route. Dog on dog's good 'nough for me."

"Are you drunk? Insane? A little of each?"

"Oh, for Chrissakes!"

"Let me set you straight, you filthy hick. I'm going to be married. I don't mess around, not anymore, not with you, not with anybody. And if you weren't his best friend I'd kick you bowlegged and claw your eyes out. You're pathetic, you know that? Disgusting! Now, get out of here! Out!"

A knock at the door froze the two of them.

"It's me, dearest. Somebody in there with you?"

Striding past Raider, she unlocked the door and swung it wide. "Only your friend. Who has just, believe it or not, propositioned me. Offered me two 'whole dollars cash money.' I politely asked him to leave."

"Doc," began Raider lamely. "She's mixin' it all up. I was just tryin' to prove to you—"

It was as far as he got. Up came Doc's right, crashing into his jaw, sending him tangle-legged against the bed and down onto it. Down Doc came on top of him, flailing away, smashing him three, four good shots to the head. Raising his knees, Raider pushed him off, rolled off the bed, thumped to the floor, and jumped up spryly. Doc, too, was up, back to the attack, absolutely furious.

"Bastard! Stinking son of a bitch! Dirty, rotten, slimy . . ."

Raider's left stopped his mouth abruptly, snapping his head back.

"I don't wanna fight you, Doc, buddy. Don' make me. Please! You're makin' me. Don't, Doc!"

Toe to toe they went at it. A hard left dented Raider's ribs, setting him caterwauling in pain. And responding with a left of his own that found the side of Doc's head. Almost immediately his ear became as red as Lydia-Mae's dress. She had backed against the wall at the first blow, round-eyeing the two of them.

She suddenly stopped gasping and found her voice. "Stop it! Stop it!"

She might as well have been talking to two wild steers. Neither paid her the slightest attention. Doc knocked Raider flat, stepped over him, waggling his hand and the pain out of his knuckles, and, standing in the hallway, picked him up, propped him against the doorjamb, and swung. Unfortunately, Raider's knees buckled, and he started slipping just as Doc's right came at his head. It arrived too late, missing his crown and bashing against solid wood.

"Owwwwwwww!"

Raider shook out the cobwebs and returned his attention to Doc's ribs, belting him huffing and puffing up the hall. At the landing, holding a fistful of shirtfront with one hand, Raider reared back with the other, driving a haymaker forward. Doc ducked, slipping to one side, and Raider followed his fist down the stairs, clattering to rest at the bottom. Doc raced down, jumped nimbly over him, pivoted, and bent over, intent on applying the finishing blow. Instead he got a shot full in the face that sent him reeling backwards, flopping over the arm of an overstuffed chair upside down on the cushion, his body bunched like a sack of grain. For a split second he teetered, then completed his fall, landing on his feet on the floor on the opposite side.

Raider came at him cursing. Doc reached for a convenient potted palm and, wielding it like a wagon tongue, smashed Raider in the head with dirt and roots, staggering him.

Through the lobby they battled, screaming imprecations at each other. Loungers jumped up from their chairs to make a path for them, watching, cheering, applauding enthusiastically, whistling.

"Kill the son of a bitch!"

"Beat him to death!"

"Let's see some goddamn blood!"

"Bust his fuckin' skull!"

"Mercy, don't hurt each other."

Raider sent Doc crashing through the matching front doors out onto the verandah. Up on his feet with surprising quickness for one so battered and bloodied, Doc sidestepped the follow-up punch, permitting Raider to pass him and teeter briefly on the edge of the top step. Then Doc sent him crashing down to the sidewalk with a magnificently timed, expertly placed wallop from his uninjured left. By now his right, having smashed against the doorjamb, was swollen to twice normal size.

"Had enough?" he bellowed.

Raider answered, lurching up the steps after him. Doc flew past. Raider turned and gave chase. He caught up with him halfway across the street and decked him with a one-two punch to the ribs that could be clearly heard at either end of the street.

"Stop it! Stop it!"

It was Lydia-Mae, coming out onto the verandah. If either heard her, he gave no indication. Duty called and was promptly answered. Doc slammed a flurry of lefts to

Raider's head and one right; he howled in pain, cursing himself for neglecting to remind himself not to use it. Raider came back at him with a driving right to the eye that started it closing almost at once.

By now, so exhausted were both, having effectively reduced one another to twin piles of bone, blood, and pain, they could hardly remain upright and swing their arms. They did so, but more slowly with every punch, until by the time they reached the front doors of the Bucket of Blood, directly opposite the hotel, they looked like two bloodied, man-sized marionettes being manipulated in slow motion. Only their eyes reflected their determination to continue. Each stared fiercely at the other, and the distinct possibility that it was to be a fight to the death encouraged the onlookers outside the Bucket of Blood to cheer themselves hoarse.

They slugged their way inside, missing four punches for every one that landed. And those that did could be compared in power, authority, and impact with the petting of a faithful dog. Between blows, each lay against the other for support while catching their breaths. Then they separated again, swung and missed anew, or struck each other wholly by chance, inasmuch as the blood streaming down their faces all but completely blinded them. Quickly exhausting themselves, they would again fall against each other in an inverted V, bleeding, bursting with pain, and mumbling curses.

Doc's right hand looked like five fat pink sausages, the left side of his chest was all but completely caved in from earlier hammer blows to his rib cage, his right cheek was broken, his left swollen, the eye above it puffed like a pillow and sealed tightly shut. Twin freshets of blood coursed from his nose, his knees wobbled ominously, and his remaining available breath came in little staccato gasps that suggested both lungs were on the verge of collapse.

Raider appeared equally fit. Both cheeks looked to be shattered, or at the very least, fractured. His jawbone sagged in its sack of flesh, suggesting that a well-placed shot had unhinged one side of it. He leaned heavily to his left, like a man with one leg shorter than the other, in deference to five cracked ribs. His left-hand knuckles were scrambled, his thumb dislocated, and his right was gloved with blood and hung from his wrist as limp as a dead fish. Pain consumed him from ankles to hairline, and, like his adversary, a high percentage of the blood his veins carried he now wore on the outside.

Standing toe to toe in the middle of the floor, they parted, swung, missed, and fell on their faces, heads to feet. They lay motionless, unheeding the loud accolade produced by their audience. Lydia-Mae burst through the doors.

"Dear God in heaven! He's dead! They're both dead!" And having delivered this blunt opinion, she promptly burst into tears.

Death, however, does not come easily to men as alive as Raider and Doc. Pain, yes; injury, definitely; discomfort, interior breakage, bruises and abrasions, most assuredly. But within sixty seconds of the combatants' simultaneous collapse and the end of the battle of the Bucket of Blood they were unceremoniously picked up, conveyed outside, and dumped one upon the other into the horse trough. This not only revived them, sputtering and alternately groaning and cursing, but washed off most of the blood, requiring their hearts to pump forth a fresh new application to the afflicted areas.

Their revival had a surprising effect upon Lydia-Mae. Her initial heartfelt concern over their well-being immediately gave way to an entirely different reaction.

"Idiots! Morons! Stupid jackasses! Weatherbee, I should jilt you flat, you, you, you . . ."

Doc only half heard her. Like his partner, he was preoccupied, devoting his full concentration to suffering and bleeding.

CHAPTER TWO

A local doctor tended to the more serious wounds of both operatives. Luckily, neither was as badly hurt as each declared himself to be. Over the course of the next two days, neither would speak to the other, despite Lydia-Mae's repeated insistence to Doc to "shape up and shake hands." Time's passing had given her a new perspective on Raider and the motive underlying his two-dollar proposition to her.

"I really don't think he dislikes me as much as he does the idea of you two breaking up. He didn't proposition me to proposition me, he just wanted to test my virtue. Find out if I meant what I've promised. Test me. For you."

"You're being much too generous, what he wanted was to discredit you. Let's not talk about him. On top of all my aches and pains, it makes me sick to my stomach."

Doc lay on the bed bandaged, broken, balmed, but no longer bleeding, and his hitherto securely sealed eye was beginning to open. Lydia-Mae sat beside him, supporting herself with her arms against the inch-thick mattress. Lowering her mouth to his, she kissed him ardently, finding the tip of his tongue with her own.

"Oh, God, don't do that," he spluttered, tearing his mouth free.

"You don't like it?"

"It's what it's doing to me." He flung the sheet aside, revealing his battered, naked body. His cock was firming,

21

rising to full erection, its pinkness deepening into a vivid purple.

"Oh, my," she cooed admiringly.

The tip of her tongue found the center of his upper lip, laving it gently. She glanced back at the door, got up, assured herself that it was locked, returned, and, smiling, dropped slowly to her knees.

"Ohhhhhhh," moaned Doc.

"Please, I haven't even started. Or don't you want me to?"

"Ohhhhhhh."

She laughed lightly, a lilting singsong. She licked her full, sensuous lips and brought them down to his throbbing cockhead. Out flashed her tongue, licking it lightly, savoring it.

"Yummy yum yum."

"Ohhhhhhh."

For fully three minutes she tongue-lashed his head, setting his helpless balls pounding furiously, filling, hammering like each had a ballpeen hammer inside.

"Ohhhhhhh."

She started down his cock, her burning lips barely touching it. And when by chance they did, she would widen them to avoid contact. Down, down, down.

"Ohhhhhhh."

And up, up, up. And down. All the way to the base. And into a new phase, working her tongue round and around his cock, swirling, laving, thrashing it mercilessly. Then whipping her mouth free, leaving it erect, pulsing, threatening to burst, to issue forth a load so copious, so powerfully projected, it would surely geyser six feet in the air.

She turned to licking his balls, setting them silently rumbling. She ran her agile and tireless tongue round and around them, up the valleys of his crotch, around the root of his cock, tip-traveling slowly upward to his head, pouncing on it, gobbling it, devouring it, freeing his load.

"Ohhhhhhhhhhhhhhhhhh!"

Up came his sperm, exploding, filling her mouth, sliding easily down her throat. Freeing his head from the vise of her lips, she studied it, watching the last drop of come surface and gleam brightly. Catching it neatly on the tip of her tongue, she spread it over her upper lip, then licked it clean. A second droplet replaced the first. She caught it just as neatly, expertly. Then she began working his cock with her hand.

"What . . ."

"Sssssh! Don't talk. Don't do a thing. Just lie still."

Gently beating his cock into shape, into renewed erection, she stood up and flung off her skirt. Mounting him, she seized his cock and guided it into her wet quim.

"Ohhhhhhh."

She began slowly gyrating, then faster, faster still, bouncing and bucking wildly, wantonly. The bed was creaking loudly beneath their combined weight. Doc stared. She had caught fire, gasping loudly, eyes bulging from their sockets, romping, rough-riding him like a skilled hand on a bucking bronco. Up, down, around, driving, pounding.

Again he came, his balls screaming, come shooting upward, splattering her burning cunt, flooding, filling it.

"Ohhhhhhh."

Raider lay on his bed in the room directly above Doc and Lydia-Mae's, under a sheet, unclothed, in continuing mortal pain. And cursing himself for his failure to kill his partner.

"Which maybe woulda been goin' a little far, but it'd sure 'nough save him from throwin' his life away on that she-bitch-whore! Better to fuckin' die with honor than to live with dis."

Dis? Could that be used as short for dishonor? Never having gotten past the fourth grade—he had dropped out of school at ten—he wouldn't know. Mr. College-Education would.

"College education, shit!" He cackled and winced. "Sure as hell doesn't do a body any good toe to toe. Ha! I beat him proper, damn if I didn't. Hell, if I hadn'ta slipped and fell like I did I'da likely killed the son of a bitch!"

He tried to rise, got halfway up, and sank back with a

pitiful groan. Taking a deep, painful breath, he tried a second time and succeeded. Easing his legs over the side, he attacked the bowl of tepid chicken soup she had brought him. Tepid it had been last time he tried it. Cold now. Picking up the spoon and bending over it, he lifted a quantity and attempted to pour it between his lips. He struggled to part them to admit it against the excruciating discomfort of his aching jaw, which she had obligingly and expertly re-hinged for him shortly after he was pulled out of the horse trough in order to prevent Doc underneath him from drowning.

Doc.

"Go ahead an' marry her, you asshole! Go ahead! Stick your turkey neck into the noose. Let her jerk it tight. Clamp the knot against your jugular. Kick an' dance an' gurgle an' choke to death. Hearts an' flowers, sixteen kids, an' a wife that's laying for half the town—for which you'll be grateful as hell, bein' as somebody's got to put bread on the table."

He could only speak through clenched teeth. Unclenching them would trigger immediate, certain disaster, unhinging his jaw and bringing on an agony that would render his present pain trifling by comparison. He tried again and managed to get a third of a spoonful of soup into his mouth; the other two-thirds dribbled down his chin. It tasted delicious, despite its coldness. Enough of it into his maw would restore his energy, speed his healing, lessen his pain, and eventually cure him entirely. The prospect appealed. If he got lucky and got on his feet before Doc, he could waylay the bastard in his bed and finish the job.

His conscience twinged as her face appeared on the screen of his mind. He had been hard on her, but she had forgiven him. She hadn't said she did, but her actions indicated it. Besides bringing him the soup, she had reset his jaw, and after the doctor had left, she had given him a backrub. She hadn't smiled, hadn't said a single friendly word, only yes and no and roll over, but when she left he felt a hundred percent better. Well, fifteen percent.

Was he all wrong about her? Was she as right for Doc as *he* figured she was?

"Can a polecat turn into a bird-o'-paradise? Hell no! Ooooooo!"

To be sure, there was a first time for everything, or so some folks claimed. Maybe she could reverse the natural order of things and become a good, loyal, and virtuous wife. He had failed to break them up. Still, he had one last chance—at the wedding itself, when the preacher stopped and asked if there was anyone who knew any reason why these two people shouldn't be joined. Then and there he would shove in his oar. Any reason would do. He couldn't very well say, Reverend, this man can't marry this woman on account she's a whore. Still, there must be something else, some other reason. It didn't necessarily have to be genuine. How about saying she can't marry him because she's already hitched. To who?

"How's about Sam Bass? One name's as good as another. Of course, then they'd check an' find out I'm lyin' in my teeth, an' everything'd get back on the track, an' they'd wind up gettin' married anyways. Goddamn Sam an' Bertha!"

Three days later both Raider and Doc were sufficiently recovered to be up and about. Both persisted in refusing to speak, however, and when they chanced to pass each other in the lobby, were it not for Lydia-Mae's presence, hostilities would likely have broken out anew. Raider was climbing the verandah steps late that afternoon when Doc and his fiancée emerged from the hotel.

"Bastard," muttered Raider.

"Stop it—" started Lydia-Mae.

"Jackass!" murmured Doc.

"—this—"

"Who you callin' jackass, bastard!"

"—instant!"

"Who you calling bastard, jackass!"

"Both of you!"

Heads turned on the necks of loungers in the verandah chairs. Raider and Doc were suddenly nose to nose. Both still exhibited the scars of their previous combat, but their juices and dander were up, and both seemed oblivious to their lingering aches and pains. An elderly gentleman in a battered beaver hat with a full beard generously spattered with tobacco juice pointed at the street with his walking stick.

"There go Sam Bass and Joel Collins. Back in town, I see."

Raider turned, focusing on the two arrivals and fixing them in mind forever. It was the first time either he or Doc had ever seen them. What a break, he thought.

"Amen," he said. "Let's go get 'em."

"Easy, easy," said Doc, laying a friendly, restraining hand on his shoulder. "No hurry. They'll be back to stay for a while. Let's do it right."

Lydia-Mae seized both their arms, marched them down the steps, and steered them up the street out of earshot of the people on the verandah. By now Bass and Collins were well down the street.

"You listen to me, you two dimwits. Don't you go messing around with Bass and Collins. You'll end up getting your heads blown off!"

Doc sighed audibly. "Lydia, dear heart, we've been all over this. You know why we're here, what we have to do."

"Take those two in," said Raider. "Dead or alive. Preferably the former."

"Dead is what you'll be!" shrilled Lydia-Mae irritably.

"Ssssh! For heaven's sakes, keep it down," blurted Doc.

She impulsively threw her arms around him. "Doc, darling, please forget about them. Can't you tell your superiors they never showed up? They've gone away, you don't know where, and . . . and somebody else'll have to find them?"

Raider chuckled coldly. "Old A.P. would purely love to hear that. Mr. Flasharity here wouldn't have to quit; he'd get himself canned proper."

"That suits me!" snapped Lydia.

Doc frowned wearily. "Not me. Let's go, Rade."

They left Lydia-Mae bawling threats at them, stamping her foot angrily, shaking her small fist. They followed the two arrivals at a half trot, not wanting to draw attention to their interest, but not wanting to lose sight of them either. Which they eventually did, turning the corner just in time to catch them entering their place. They could hear a muffled spontaneous greeting from within as the door closed behind them.

"Makes me sick how popular bastards like them are 'mongst their kind," observed Raider. "What now?"

Doc surveyed the sky. "We've still got four or five hours till dark. I say we keep an eye on the place until it's good and dark."

"Bullshit! I'm in no shape to stand around like a cigar store Indian eyeballin' that door, waitin' for stars an' moon. Better we drop it for the meantime, go 'bout our business, an' come back here say nine o'clock. You can go back to your lovey-dovey an' catch up on your spoonin'."

"Try minding your own beeswax, Raider, for just once in your life."

"You *are* my beeswax, mister. We're still a team, till this thing's wrapped up an' in the journal. So don' go lettin' yourself get too distracted."

Doc grinned. "You know something? I believe you're jealous! You are, aren't you?"

"Oh, hell yes. Green with envy, that's me. I mean whores are 'bout as scarce round these parts as a bull in a belfry."

"Don't start—"

"Oh, go fuck yourself. On second thought, don't. No need to go makin' her nibs jealous."

With this he waved and started walking off. Doc stood seething, debating whether or not to catch up with him and tap him once. Just once. Punishment for his snideness. Unfortunately, he didn't feel up to it physically. He watched him limp away, favoring his left side and his aching, court-plastered ribs. Doc snickered.

"The shape he's in, one shot to his brisket would probably kill him."

Lydia-Mae persisted in alternately threatening and pleading with Doc to stay away from Bass. His patience finally exhausted, he stormed out of the hotel and began saloon-hopping in quest of his partner. Festivities in Deadwood did not await the onset of darkness. There was no clock on drinking, romping, and carousing; it was virtually nonstop, solely dependent upon the stamina of the participants. As a rule, things did get reasonably quiet between six and eight in the morning, but shortly thereafter, the general carrying-on would break out afresh, and the noon hour saw as many drunks, wounded, and dead on the streets as midnight, albeit a different cast of characters.

Doc disliked Deadwood with an intensity approaching Raider's. Preparing to enter Montana, a shot whistled over his head, causing him to duck and bump his still tender nose soundly against one of the doors, then catch the tip of it between them as they swung back.

"Owwww!"

In he ventured, rubbing his nose, drawing curious stares from barflies and table occupants alike. He spotted Raider at the end of the bar hoisting a tumblerful of whiskey, undoubtedly Rookus Juice. How with his weak stomach he could stomach the sulphuric acid that crossed mahogany from Frisco to Fort Smith, Arkansas, under said name was more than Doc had ever been able to fathom. Vile though it was, it was his favorite.

"What are you drinking?" he asked. "As if I didn't know."

"Valley Tan, otherwise knowed as Shanahan's Domestic Whiskey. I asked the man for Rookus Juice but he's fresh out. I hate this town. What's up? See anythin' of our friends?"

"I haven't been looking."

"I been thinkin'. What do you say we drop the hanky-panky, march into that shithole bold as brass, ask to see them, get the drop on 'em, march 'em the hell out . . ."

"You always were one for clever strategy."

The piano player struck up "Sweet Betsy From Pike," joined by a chorus of voices, off-key, off-rhythm, unnecessarily loud and offensive.

"Pretty," commented Raider. "Always like 'Betsy.'"

"Drink up, Rade, and let's go."

"You on the wagon? Buy yourself a drink, why don' you? Let's see the color o' my money."

"Our pay should have been here today. Tomorrow for sure. You'll get every cent I owe you."

"Plus twenty percent interest."

"Ten."

"Twenty!"

"Ten! We shook on it."

Raider started to dismiss him with a wave and a sour look, then paused, finished his whiskcy, and ordered another. Doc ordered Bingham's five-year-old reserve Scotch, thirty-five cents an ounce, prompting Raider to express his opinion of both his taste and extravagance. The object of his scorn pretended not to hear him. They drank in silence.

"Doc . . ."

"Mmmmmm."

"Are you really, honest-to-God goin' to marry her?"

"Just drink. See if you can make yourself sick."

"I'm serious."

"So am I."

The doors opened and in walked Sam Bass. He was built like a flour barrel above the waist, his upper arm muscles all but splitting the seams of his coat. He walked jauntily, his homely face fixed with a permanent look of scorn. Around his bull neck hung a rawhide lanyard bound by an expensive-looking gold clasp. He wore his Stetson on the back of his head, lending his rectangular forehead the appearance of a brick shoved into a slot between his eyebrows and his hairline. He wore no facial hair.

"Ornery lookin' bastard, isn' he?" observed Raider."

"Ssssh!"

"Come struttin' in like a fat old rooster, like he owns the place."

Bass swaggered by without looking at either of them. Heading toward the piano, he was stopped by a well-shaped brunette who reined him into conversation.

Doc frowned. "I wonder where his partner is?"

"In his pocket. Seriously, how 'bout we follow him out an' see?"

"No. How many times do I have to tell you? We wait until dark."

• • •

Doc went back to the hotel to placate Lydia-Mae and dine with her. He rejoined Raider at the appointed time, checking his Waterbury watch against the clock in the window of Heatherington & Wilshire's Jewelry Store. Raider read the Big Dipper circling the North Star as nine and arrived at the spot they had occupied earlier, across the street from the newly painted two-story frame house, two minutes after Doc.

"They're both in there," he said. "I followed his nibs home after you left Montana."

"Rade..."

"Don' worry, he's not onto me. Not unless a little bird tol' him we come to town." He grinned devilishly and winked.

"Shut your mouth or I'll shut it for you!"

Raider grunted and smirked. They stood waiting for two hours, watching the passersby, listening to the town. Doc repeatedly consulted his watch, to Raider's growing irritation. At five after eleven a familiar figure could be seen approaching.

"Thank God you haven't done anything foolish yet!" rasped Lydia-Mae. "Thank God I got here before you could. Doc Weatherbee, my mind's made up. You're coming home with me, and right now!"

"The hell he is!" burst Raider.

"You keep out of this."

"Lydia, sweetheart, go back to the hotel."

"Not without you. Either you come or we're quits. I mean it, it'll be all over."

"Don' go back!" shot Raider.

"Shut up and mind your own business!" exclaimed Doc.

Raider obliged. He stood watching and listening to them argue. Doc stood by his guns. Lydia-Mae finally threw up her hands and stalked off, as angry as a slapped hornet, observed Raider.

"That does it," he chuckled. "You're off the hook. You won't have to marry her after all."

"Put a cork in it and let's go. I'm fed up standing around.

It could be noon tomorrow before those two come out. Even then, who says they'll be together. Let's go in and take them."

"Now you're talkin'!"

The decision was hasty, spawned of impulse induced by anger, and risky at best. Entering the place, it occurred to Doc that the worst that could happen would be for them to come upon one or the other outlaw, but not both.

Which was exactly what happened. The gambling casino portion of the establishment occupied the entire ground floor. Roulette wheels whirled, dice danced in chuck-a-luck cages, cards were softly shuffled and dealt. A single faro table in one corner attracted four players and a large knot of kibitzers, the clicking of the casekeeper vying with that of the roulette balls. The place was mobbed and filled as well with smoke, babble, and a singularly out-of-place touch of dignity in the person of three formally attired musicians, two of them sawing away on violin and cello respectively, the third fingering the piano through a classical selection Doc was unable to identify.

The bar stretched from corner to corner across the rear; above it was hung the biggest mirror by several feet Raider had ever seen above any bar anywhere. No fewer than four bartenders busied themselves behind the mahogany, and every foot of brass rail supported a foot, except for spaces as wide as a man reserved at the extreme left and right for the floor waiters to place their drink orders.

Raider nodded toward the nearest roulette table. Sam Bass, wearing a gold-braided maroon silk vest over shirt-sleeves, a string tie, custom-fitted trousers, and handsome hand-tooled boots, stood watching the roulette wheel. A tall, emaciated, hollow-and-pitted cheeked, middle-aged individual, determinedly belaboring a chaw of tobacco, his slender hands quivering with palsy, stood beside him, whispering into his ear.

"I wonder if that's Collins standing with him?" murmured Doc.

"Can't be. Too old."

"Welcome, gentlemen, welcome."

A red-nosed man with thinning blond hair equally divided along the center of his scalp and plastered down on both sides approached them, his hand extended.

"May I have your six-gun please, sir?" he asked Raider amiably.

Raider shot a glance at Doc, whose own .38 Diamondback reposed in a shoulder holster under his left armpit and under his jacket.

"Policy of the house," persisted the man. "You'll get it back when you leave, of course."

"We're lookin' for Mr. Collins," said Raider, ignoring his request and outstretched hand.

"Your gun, if you don't mind." Cold authority replaced the friendly tone.

"Is that Mr. Collins standing next to Mr. Bass?" inquired Doc.

The man turned. "No. Look, fella..."

Raider drew with the quickness of a rattler seizing a helpless mouse and jammed the muzzle of his Colt hard against their welcomer's ample belly.

"Shut up!"

"Rade..." began Doc wearily.

Raider ignored him. His drawing had attracted the attention of everyone within thirty feet of them. Including Bass. He came swaggering over.

"Mr. Bass?" Raider slowly shifted his aim to him. "We'd like to invite you to step outside, you an' your partner. Where is the son of a bitch?"

"What the hell do you think you're doing, cowboy? Put that thing away before you hurt somebody. Before you get your head blown off!"

Raising his hand, he snapped his fingers. Raider followed the action. In line with it and beyond it he spotted a man crouched behind the upstairs railing, the rifle in his hand aimed squarely at him.

Raider fired.

The man fired. His shot went awry, shattering a roulette wheel as he slumped to one side and lay still. Instantly, all hell broke loose. Within seconds the two Pinkertons had scrambled behind an overturned poker table, chips and cards spilling to the floor. Raider sneaked a peek out his side, drawing two quick blasts from two rifles he couldn't even see. Women screamed, men bellowed; Bass roared, cursed, and threatened. He stood in the midst of the melee waving his powerful arms, demanding attention and quiet and getting neither. Raider took careful aim at him. Doc grabbed his arm.

"Don't, for God's sakes! Him we want alive. What in God's name ever possessed you—"

A rifle shot splintering a hole midway between them stopped him. He gulped, lowered his head, peered around his side of the table, got off two quick ones, and dropped a second balcony marksman in his tracks. Raider got the third and last, who was foolishly standing at the railing, loading his weapon. Over he fell, plunging straight down twenty feet and smashing the top of his head against the hardwood floor. Doc watched and winced.

"If that son of a bitch is still breathing, my hat's off to him," remarked Raider.

"Shut up, you stupid hothead!" snapped Doc. "Every time I try to work dangerous things out the easiest, best, least risky way, you have to mess everything up!"

Raider cut him off, grabbing his arm. "Look!"

Bass was fleeing, running up the stairs. They hurried him along with shots at his heels. Gaining the landing, he raced down it and through the door at the end. His three riflemen having been summarily dispatched, the battle ended abruptly, inasmuch as everyone else present had turned in their arms at the door in compliance with "the policy of the house." Raider and Doc slowly rose to their feet.

"It's all over, folks," announced Raider. "Anybody disagrees gets himself just what those three dead-eye Dicks upstairs got, savvy? You!"

He turned to the red-nosed man who had demanded his gun. The man's hands were high and trembling, his face bleached with fear.

"D-d-don't sh-sh-shoot!"

"Those two up there together?" The man nodded. "Okay, lead the way."

"Rade!" snapped Doc in astonishment. "What are you doing? You go up there, you'll be walking straight into an ambush."

"Sure, but with a shield. Come here, you."

"Doc . . ."

So weak was the voice behind them it was barely distinguishable above the mumbling and murmuring of the crowd. Both turned slowly, Raider holding his iron leveled at the man's gut. Behind them, just inside the door, lay Lydia-Mae, a shawl over her shoulders, a crimson spot the size of a silver dollar in her chest.

CHAPTER THREE

Raider shoved the man ahead of him through the door. The upstairs room was empty. It had been converted into an office, complete with desk, Sears, Roebuck four-wheeled safe, and a four-drawer wooden file cabinet. The window to the left of the safe was wide open, the breeze fluttering the curtains and setting them dancing. Shoving his shield aside and sending him tumbling into a corner, Raider rushed to the window so fast that, reaching the sill, he had to grab the frame to keep from smashing his face against the upraised casement and flying out. Leaning out, he could hear the faint rumbling of hooves, fading, fading, fading into silence.

"Son of a bitch!"

It was at least a twenty-foot drop to the ground, but they had made it, and so could he. Scrambling onto the sill, he flashed a parting glare at his shield cowering in the corner and jumped. He landed hard, twisting his left ankle slightly, which prompted a full thirty-second string of curses. Rubbing the affected area, he glanced about. An unsaddled mare stood tethered to a fence post. Without a second's hesitation, out of instinct born of years of experience, keen, instantaneous judgment, and the ability to fit available resources to the needs of the moment, he promptly stole the horse. Seconds later he was thundering off in the direction taken by Bass and Collins.

A half-moon surrounded by a million stars ignited the heavens. The night wind was up, flattening the front brim of his J.B. against the crown, plugging his nostrils, slamming against his face as he bent low and urged the mare forward. The ground was tricky—uneven and studded with stones—but she was surefooted and eager to run. Run she did, as his heels dug into her barrel, urging her forward.

"Run, lady, run! Run, run! Good girl."

Good horse, he mused, fleetingly wondering who she belonged to. Hopefully, the big-mouthed, red-nosed man at the door. He snickered. He had sure enough loosened his bowels this night! For the small satisfaction that gave.

Bass and Collins were heading east toward Fort Meade. With any luck he'd catch up with them before the Chicago & Northwest Railroad main tracks. With no luck, they'd cut north or south long before the tracks. They were, he estimated, at least a mile ahead.

He reached the tracks shortly; there was no sign of Bass and Collins.

"Bastards!"

He'd lost them. It wasn't so much definite knowledge that he had as instinct. A man chasing *felt* when his quarry had gotten away from him. He felt it now, cursed it, denied it, and, tightening his face, tried to drive it out of mind; but it stayed, haunting and convincing him. Reining left, he began circle-searching. Any light he saw he would investigate. Damn! If only he knew what their horses looked like.

His thoughts went back to the gambling casino and Lydia-Mae lying in Doc's arms, the spot on her chest slowly enlarging. She was still breathing when he'd left the two of them to hasten upstairs, managing a sad, weak smile as if to assure Doc that it wasn't as bad as it looked. But it *was* a bad hit, a bad place; the shot has missed her heart and gone into her lung. Painful. Dangerous as hell. And Doc. Holding and comforting her, the expression on his face had wrenched Raider's heart in his chest. It was abject helplessness shadowed with fear and dread.

"Get a doctor to her. Get that damned thing outta her. She's young, strong. With any luck . . ."

He sighed. Nothing was quite as useless, as unworthy

of even passing consideration as futile hope. Why had she followed them? As near as he could make out, she was the only one hit, apart from the three sharpshooters upstairs.

Why in God's name did it have to be her!

Lydia-Mae had been carried to Dr. Hannibal Watts's office upstairs over Heatherington and Wilshire's Jewelry Store. Watts had treated both Pinkertons earlier, and Doc had every confidence in his ability to keep Lydia-Mae alive. Every confidence and all the wishful thinking he could muster. The doctor was a little man, barely five feet tall and under 110 pounds. His booming voice was almost absurdly ill suited to his unprepossessing appearance. He was slightly deaf and cupped his ear with his left hand in preference to using a cumbersome trumpet. Doc sat on a stool in a corner of the low-ceilinged, cramped little combination office, examining room, and operating room, watching Watts work in silence. He averted his glance when the doctor went in after the slug. He returned his eyes only after hearing the telltale clink of lead dropping into a basin. He watched as Watts worked feverishly to stanch the blood released by the recovered slug. He did so and bandaged the wound. Lydia-Mae slept on.

"She'll be coming outta the chloroform in half an hour or so," boomed Watts.

Up on his feet, Doc approached him. He smoothed Lydia-Mae's hair back from her forehead. "What are her chances?"

Watts shrugged. Doc blanched. Watts smiled thinly. "Take it easy, young fella. I never give out odds. I *will* say I think she'll make it. She's lost a lotta blood, most of it back at that shebang, but she's young, strong, healthy. And strikes me as a fighter. Some fight harder than others; she's a fighter. You believe in God?"

"Yes."

"I don't. But if you do, don't be afraid to get in touch with him. They say if you believe he'll listen, he will. I can't do any more for her now. She's in his, in somebody's hands." He began rolling down his sleeves.

"You're not leaving!"

"No point in staying. You can if you like." Watts consulted his watch. He checked it, wound it, and pocketed it. "Going on for midnight. I'm missing my beauty sleep. Relax, young fella, she'll be okay."

"You're sure of that?"

He bristled. "Hell no! How can I be? I'm only a doctor, not your friend upstairs." He softened his tone and expression. "Frettin' won't help her a lick. When she wakes up, better she see a smile on your face." He half laughed. "You should start practicin'. Good night. Good luck."

Dawn rosied the eastern sky. The air was damp and still. Raider yawned, began working his neck, rolling his head in a circle, yawned again, tasted last night's liquor, listened to his stomach rumble, pulled up, dismounted, took a leak in the tall grass, got back on the mare, and started back toward Deadwood.

The sun was yellowing the sky, clearing the horizon, and starting its ascent when he rode in. Returning the mare to her post behind Bass and Collins's place, he walked to the jewelry store and up the side stairs, continuing to favor his long-suffering ribs. Dr. Watts and Doc were standing at the table, Lydia-Mae stretched out on it smiling, as pale as ivory, mused Raider worriedly.

"They got away."

Doc frowned. "We can see that."

"How's she doin'? How you doin', ah...Lydia?"

The last syllable was no sooner out of his mouth than she began choking. Her cheeks reddened, and blood gushed from her mouth.

"Jesus!" boomed Watts.

Doc bent over her and kissed her lightly, his hands flying about helplessly in complete and utter frustration.

"Sweetheart, sweetheart."

Standing in the doorway, his hand on the knob, Raider watched and consciously suffered as the blood continued to pour out of her mouth, sending a gleaming stream down the side of her jaw. She stiffened, gasping softly, choked again, and slowly closed her eyes. Her head lolled to one side.

"Lydia!" burst out Doc.

Watts was suddenly holding him back from her with one arm as best he could. Raider strode forward. He stopped and stood awkwardly looking from one to the other. Doc had stepped back from her. He appeared thunderstruck, his hands against his cheeks, his eyes wide. For a moment he seemed incapable of moving. Then, backing off further, he sank slowly down onto the stool. Raider went to him.

"Easy, Doc."

He didn't hear. He had fled, dispatching his mind from his body. His eyes were fixed on her face, staring dully. Watts shook his head at Raider, then went to a cabinet and poured a glass of liquor for Doc. Doc waved it away.

"It's all right, all right."

"I'm sorry," said Watts.

"You did your best."

"I . . . gave you hope. I shouldn't have. I had no right . . ."

Doc shook his head, stopping further words. Slowly he got up, went to the table, kissed her lightly, and covered her face with the sheet.

"What do I owe you, Doctor?"

"Nothing, I . . ."

"Come on, Rade. Let's go."

CHAPTER FOUR

In all their years together Raider had never known Doc so desolate, so painfully crushed. Seeing him in such a state confirmed his now firm belief that he had indeed been crazy about Lydia-Mae. In love deep as the ocean, wide as the sky. By nature Doc was a lonely man, as lonely as Raider. Over the years the two had been partners, Doc had dallied with countless women, offered attention and affection to a score or more, and slept with hundreds. Raider had seen him lose his heart and head, and eventually the object of his ardor, for one reason or another many times.

But he had never seen him take it nearly as hard as this. He appeared stunned, the reaction of one immediately following a tragedy, a reaction that usually wore off within the hour, replaced by grief. But his bewilderment, his shock did not wear off this time. He kept his eyes down, unwilling to raise his head. He could not speak above a whisper, and when he did react, it was not in words so much as grunts and incoherent muttering. He seemed oblivious to everything going on around him, including Raider's presence. He had removed himself from the scene and now occupied a kind of private limbo which put no demands upon his senses and permitted neither distraction nor relief from his suffering.

He refused to start a conversation, refused to continue one started by Raider. On the morning of the second day after Lydia's death, Raider gave up trying.

"He'll be back," he assured himself. "It takes time."

Their pay had arrived from Chicago, but Raider did not dun his partner for the money he had borrowed. It could wait; everything could, even Bass and Collins, until after the funeral. Raider fervently hoped that seeing her casket lowered into the ground, the handful of dirt ceremoniously tossed down onto it, the funeral ended, Doc would come away from the cemetery altered in mood, moved into the second stage of mourning, into grief and bitterness capped by resolve: Mount up, ride out, and find the two outlaws. Activity would help him as much as time passing.

Fittingly, it rained the day of the funeral. No deluge, only a gentle shower, just enough to gray the day and with it the occasion, and dampen everyone's spirits even more than they already were. Most of the mourners were working girlfriends from Bass and Collins's brothel, Raider noted as he stood at the graveside alongside Doc, listening to the drops pelt their hats, watching them pock and pit the mound of freshly turned earth on the opposite side of the grave. Lydia's friends were appropriately attired in black and were all tearful, saddened, and sniffling.

When the minister, standing under an umbrella held by Dr. Watts, finished and closed his Bible and the knot of people loosened, one of the women approached Raider. Leaving Doc and Dr. Watts, he moved off with her under the protection of her umbrella.

"My name's Ella-Sue Buggs. My professional name's Sequin."

"Mmmmm."

"Her an' me was friends."

"Mmmmm."

She was no more than an inch shorter than Raider, with a narrow, pretty face, an impressive chest, and large, luminous, sad eyes. Whether their appearance was permanent or assumed for the occasion he could only guess. He wasn't in any mood to talk, but she seemed troubled and sincere, and so he listened politely.

"Liddy and I was real close, regular cater cousins. She

was dead serious 'bout quittin' the business. She loved him dearly, poor thing. Told us all straight out."

"Mmmmm."

She produced a roll of bills from her bag. "We took us up a collection. They's 'bout seventy dollar there. To help, you know, defray the expenses an' suchlike."

All hail the heart of a whore, reflected Raider. Tears glistened, welling on her lower lids, then sliding down her powdered cheeks.

"I loved that little girl."

"I guess lotsa folks did."

"Like a baby sister. This shouldn'ta happened; crazy wild shot." Her face darkened. "Them two's as much to blame as whoever shot her. More."

Like a dry leaf skittering across an ice-locked pond a thought traversed Raider's mind.

"I bet you'd like to see the two o' them behind bars."

"Strung up's more like it!"

He brightened. "You know somethin', you an' me got us some nuts-an'-bolts talkin' to do."

"What about?"

"Bass an' Collins, what else? You must know 'em pretty good."

"Good as most o' the girls."

"Why don' you meet me in a hour in Room 3C over at the Deadwood?"

Her sad expression gave way to a pixieish grin. "You betcha! You got a dollar? I mean 'sides what I jest give you there?"

"I can scrape one up."

Putting pleasure before business at the lady's request, and with an eye to doing what he could to win her confidence, Raider stripped down to the buff and prepared to climb under the sheet to join her. He sucked in a soft whistle as he turned down the top of the sheet. Unencumbered by clothing, her breasts approached the size of ripe cantaloupes: enormous, solid, high-riding, they sported round, pink areolae the diameter of twenty-dollar double eagles.

"Heavenly day!" she exclaimed. "You sure 'nough look like you've been runned over by a wagon train. What happened?"

"Fell off a stool hangin' a picture."

"Oh. What's this you got here, the nail?" She tittered and grabbed his rapidly erecting cock. She squeezed.

"Hey, easy! Them's fragile goods."

She threw back the sheet and, holding his cock in one hand, wet the other on her tongue and slid it slowly down his length.

"It's niiice. Long, not too fat, not too lean."

"Can we save the compliments an' get down to business?"

"Suits me. How do you want it?"

"Upstairs, downstairs, an' in my lady's chamber, how you think?"

"But *how?* Missionary? Doggie? You on top? Me? Sideways? Standin' up? Sittin' in a chair? Johnny 'gainst the wall? Twist 'bout? Crosswise? Back door? Face? Wagon wheel? Under thunder?"

"Wait, wait, wait! I ain't int'rested in your life story. Missionary suits me fine. How 'bout you?"

"Heavenly day, you *are* a gentleman. You're 'nough to turn a lady's head for fair." She pecked him on the cheek. "No man never asked me how *I'd* like it afore. Missionary's just dandy."

Raider sighed inwardly. If she fucked like she talked they'd be at it till midnight. By now he was as hard as galena, thanks to her wet stroking. He mounted up, wincing slightly as his shoulder reminded him that it was not yet completely healed. Seizing his rope, she rubbed his head lightly against her quim, wetting and firing it.

"In you go, cowboy."

He didn't move. He was about to when she bucked, slamming her quim against him so hard it all but fractured his tailbone, engorging his cock, pumping, pumping, pumping, and sinking her teeth deep into his afflicted shoulder.

"Owwww! Hey, for Chrissakes!"

She bucked him off and stared in amazement. "What?"

"If you gotta chew, for Chrissakes chew the other."

"Okay."

She bucked his cock back into her and resumed. And bit deep into his other shoulder. He grimaced in pain but held his piece as she fucked on. They came together, draining every ounce of Raider's strength—but from all appearances, not a smidgen of hers. She continued fucking, gripping his back in a bear hug. He could feel himself going soft, softer. Then, to his surprise, he began to harden a second time. She bucked and bucked and bucked, bringing him back to full erection. She was breathing hard and sweating buckets, but she never broke rhythm, pushing her burning quim upward with relentless and unabating fervor, filling herself with him, draining his balls of a second, smaller load.

And a third. At which point he reckoned that his cock had not been out of her for a full five minutes. So amazing was her stamina, he began to imagine that he wouldn't reclaim it for another five. Perhaps ten? Then, abruptly, she pushed him off, scrambled about, and before he could move, even speak, all but swallowed his cock, balls and all. She sucked and sucked and sucked and sucked. It was useless. It was as limp as a well-used bar rag, and for a fleeting, terrifying moment he imagined it terminally limp, incapable of ever again erecting.

She finally gave up, bouncing up onto her knees, her cantaloupes jiggling and slapping together.

"'Smatter, you tuckered out so soon? Heavenly day! We was jest gettin' started."

"You were. I'm finished, played out, empty as a shuck, done for."

She eyed him questioningly. "You sick or somethin'?"

"Or somethin'. Can I ask you a personal question? Do you always go at it like this, I mean nonstop, practically nonbreathin'?"

"I sure 'nough gen'rally don' quit this soon. Take a sec, catch your breath." She glanced about. "Got a broom or somethin'? Gotta keep the fire goin'. You ready yet? I am."

She grabbed for his cock. He covered up, backed off, and scrambled off the bed.

"In a bit, in a bit. Jesus Christ!"

She started for him, teeth bared, eyes devilish. He held up his hands defensively. "Please! We got to talk. It's important."

"Talk now, play after?"

He gaped. "You call this play? Lady, this is work!"

"Cost you 'nother dollar. Keep goin' now it won' cost a cent."

He was climbing into his pants. "I'm gonna tell you somethin', an' you're gonna keep it a secret. Me an' Doc got to find Bass an' his pal."

"What for?"

"Ah . . . to collect some money they owe."

"You the law? You Pinkertons or such after them for stealin' that Union Pacific money?"

"What do you know 'bout that?"

"I hear things. Men talk in bed, 'specially with liquor in 'em."

"Where do you think they're headin'?"

She shrugged. "Maybe back to Texas."

"What's there?"

"That's Bass's ol' stampin' grounds. Lived down in Denton County for years an' years."

"Four years."

"You are Pinks, ain't you? Liddy never said, but the way he come to town an' sat round waitin' for you it makes sense. You don' have to say. Whatever you are, if you catch up with Bass an' Collins I'll sure 'nough raise the flag. But for the life o' me I can't 'magine what that little girl was thinkin' of. She had to be in love."

"What are you talkin' about?"

"Her fallin' in love with your partner."

"It happens."

"It does, but nothin' could come o' it, her bein' already married." His jaw dropped. "Oh, hell yes. She was Mrs. Sam Bass."

"Bullshit!"

"Was too! I oughta know. I was maid o' honor at the weddin'. Whatever was she thinkin' of, fallin' for your partner?" She paused, narrowing her eyes. "You're not gonna tell him, are you?"

"What do you think?"

CHAPTER FIVE

MR STORM SUGGESTS STRONGER EFFORT ON YOUR PART TO
LAND TWO NEW ACCOUNTS STOP IMPERATIVE YOU OBTAIN SAME
STOP ADVISE HOME OFFICE IF HELP NEEDED STOP REPORT PROG-
RESS DAILY

Doc sat at the end of the bed counting out money. He recounted it and handed it to Raider.

"Fifty, and ten dollars interest."

"Never mind the ten."

"Take it."

"Keep it."

"Suit yourself."

Raider crumpled the telegram. "What's this supposed to mean?"

"Just what it says. I may not have mentioned it, but the day before you got here I got a letter from Wagner. They're trying out a new wrinkle in communications to operatives in the field. The code book's to be shelved for everything except top-secret, complicated messages. Until further notice we correspond with innocent-looking sales inquiries and reports."

"Mr. Storm is A.P."

"Mr. Storm is also mad. Mr. Blue means he's contented as an old cow. Mr. Bright is just fine. Mr. Gray, he's a little miffed. Mr. Storm, very miffed. Mr. Flood, we seriously consider sending in our I.D.s and our resignations."

"Mr. Storm can have mine. Of all the bullshit..."

He flung the telegram into a corner. His expression of disdain belied his feelings, however. It marked the first sustained conversation he and Doc had engaged in since the funeral. He was coming back, coming out of his shell. Raider had moved into his room, bringing his bed with him over the spirited protests of the desk clerk. Doc himself wasn't all that enthusiastic over the idea, but Raider felt obligated to "keep a close eye on your helpless ass."

"I gotta ask you somethin'," he said soberly. "I don't wanna upset you, but you did tell Lydia you were a Pinkerton."

"Not right away. Only after I proposed and she accepted. We were getting married. You can't expect me to keep my job secret from my wife."

"You told her about Bass and Collins."

"She guessed, Rade. She knows what they've been up to. Everybody in Deadwood knows. This town is wide open. No law, nothing resembling it. She and all her girlfriends know those two better than you and I. She couldn't stand Bass."

"She told you that?"

"Yes. Is it so surprising?"

"Nope."

"Do you know something I don't?"

"Nope. Hey, I think I got our next move figured, which, from that telegram, we should be thinkin' about makin'. I figure they're on their way to Texas." He paused; his face darkening. "I don't like this case, Doc. It's sick in the middle an' rotten round the edges. Messy."

"Aren't they all in one way or another? But I know what you mean." He sighed. "Come on, let's pack."

The sun was wedging its fiery brilliance into the Laramie Range over the border in neighboring Wyoming when four days later, bone weary, as dry as the dust that caked their clothing, suffocatingly hot and aching, they crossed the Union Pacific tracks and the North Platte and rode into

Scotts Bluff, Nebraska. Unlike Deadwood and the many
hamlets between, Scotts Bluff was plotted as a town, not a
tilted mud slough with jerry-built and ramshackle buildings
thrown up on either side of a single street. The main street
was layered in dust three inches thick. From all appearances
it had not rained here in six weeks or more. The first sound
to reach their ears was the banging of a hammer. A sheriff's
deputy was hanging a wanted poster on the outside bulletin
board. He was gangly, toothy, homely as a snake—in Raider's offhand and unsolicited opinion. About the man's appearance Doc couldn't care less. It was the poster that
commanded his attention.

REWARD

Wells, Fargo & Co.'s office broken into and robbed by two
men, reliably identified as S. Bass and J. Collins, well-
known criminals. The company will pay

$250

for ARREST and CONVICTION of both men.

B. D'Arcy, mgr.

"Good God!" exclaimed Doc.

"What are you bitchin' for? This is the break we need.
We're on the right track."

"They'll probably hit sixteen more places before we catch
up with them. Mr. Storm's going to love this turn."

"Fuck him an' his cat."

"We owe him a wire, Rade. Four, in fact."

"We got no time."

"Howdy, boys. Jest ride in?" inquired the deputy pleas-
antly.

Raider accorded him a withering look and, dismounting,
began dusting down. "When exactly did them two hit the
office?"

"Las' night. In an' out slick as the fox in the henhouse.

Got near to ten thousand. You innerested in the ree-ward? I could sure use it, but I ain't entitled." He thumbed his badge proudly. "Sheriff's deputy."

"Any idea where they're headin'?"

"Nope. Sheriff Alzado's out with a posse turnin' over rocks. I'm holdin' the fort all by my lonesome."

The door to the sheriff's office was wide open, and the office was empty. Raider had little stomach for further conversation with Mr. Obvious. Grabbing Doc by the arm, he walked him up the street out of earshot.

"You boys beat the sheriff to it an' you'll wind up two hundred an' fifty bucks richer, you betcha," the deputy called after them. "Course they got to be convicted."

"Asshole," muttered Raider.

"Rade, I don't know about you, but I can't sit a saddle another ten feet. One more bounce'll break me in two."

"Horseshit! You're in great shape. We got to keep goin'."

"Are you serious?"

"Sssssh, Chrissakes."

"We've already covered a good three hundred miles."

"Not even two fifty."

"Raider, I don't enjoy horseback riding, not even a two-mile canter on a pleasant Sunday afternoon, much less half-way down the Great Plains in this heat in my condition. It happens I'm one of those unfortunates who, unlike youself, are not born to the saddle. Not built to it. Nature never intended me to make my home in one. It's more than uncomfortable, more than painful; it is excruciating. I ache so I can hardly walk, let alone ride. I don't need a horse, I need a doctor."

"Quit bellyachin' for Chrissakes. You're worse'n the old maid what fell down the well an' the crow shit on. Ever hear that story?"

"I have an excellent solution to the problem. They're on their way to Texas—"

"Maybe."

"They're not heading for Canada. I suggest, I demand that we board the train and ride down in comfort. Get ahead of them, get off in Big Spring and welcome them."

"Who says they're headin' for Big Spring? You don't know that. You—"

"They don't have to be. We know it's Texas. Wherever they're going we can track them by Western Union."

"Goin' by train's no good. Train wanders all over the landscape. No such thing as a direct route. We'd have to change practically every couple hours, change an' stan' aroun' the goddamn station waitin' for the next. Cost us a pretty penny. In the long run delay us somethin' fierce. We'd get to Big Spring one, maybe two days later'n if we ride. It's no good, Doc." Doc sat down on the sidewalk, wincing as his cheeks came in contact with the boards. "What are you doin'?"

"What does it look like? I'm not budging from this spot until you agree. If need be I'll sit here all night and all day tomorrow."

"You're fulla shit, you know that?"

"My decision has nothing to do with the condition of my bowels. I've said all I'm going to. What'll it be?"

Again he winced and gingerly shifted his weight to the other cheek.

Much to Raider's disappointment and indignation, after a lengthy discussion with the ticket man at the station, Doc's idea threatened to take them even farther out of their way than Raider had initially figured, zigzagging them down to the Kansas border and, from there, through a succession of changes all the way eastward to Wichita, nearly two hundred miles off the trail. In Wichita they would board the Kansas City, Mexico & Orient Railway and follow it down to Sweetwater, just over the Texas border. They would make their final change to the Texas & Pacific for the long trek southwesterly to Big Spring.

Raider took over the bellyaching, dinning his partner's ears all the way to Wichita, which they reached bird early in the morning of the third day after leaving Scotts Bluff. They stood in the station, watching a dozen crows assemble on the overhang of a warehouse loading platform.

"We're runnin' outta money."

"We're traveling free on our passes."

"I'm not talkin' about ticket cost, I mean eatin' on the run, payin' station prices for sandwiches an' such, telegrams."

"We're telegraphing collect."

"Okay, then what about all the delays? We prob'ly won't get a damn train outta here till goddamn noon. I hate trains."

"I know."

"They're dirty, they stink, all them faces starin' at you, the damn conductor bawlin' out like everybody was deaf every hundred yards, the jerkin' an' joltin', the seats. I don' know how in hell you can say a saddle is uncomfortable after ridin' these damn upholstered slabs. The drinkin' water's worse'n piss, the damn cars hotter'n the hinges o' hell, you're crowded worse'n fish in a barrel, the windows don't open so's you can breath, they're so yellow dirty you can't even see out, an' the way the rainwater collects between the panes an' sloshes back an' forth makes me sick to my stomach. You can't sleep, can't hardly doze, you gotta keep one eye open for sneak thieves lessen somebody quick hands your teeth outta your face, the damn cigar smoke's so think you can cut it into chunks, stinkin' as hell, which you don't help none lightin' up them stinkin' cheroots."

"Anything else?"

"I'm thinkin', I'm thinkin'!"

"Let's check the train."

"You do. I'm gonna get me somethin' to eat. An' check the mounts, while you're at it. Stationmaster won't likely take kindly to them standin' round his pretty platform."

He waved and sauntered off grumbling. Doc started to call him back, thought better of it, and approached the ticket window. A stern-looking, elderly woman with slightly crossed eyes framed by pinch glasses and hair that looked like blown armature wire, shooting off in a thousand different directions, stood behind the bars.

"Well?"

"Good morning."

"Is it? Spit it out, pilgrim, I got work to do."

"Lovely day, isn't it? Ahem, would you mind telling me when the next Kansas City, Mexico and Orient train is due, heading south?"

"Two-twenty."

Doc's jaw dropped. "This afternoon?"

"No, this morning."

"Not till two-twenty?"

"What did I just say? Why don't you come in here, I'll go out there, you look it up, and tell me. Would that suit Your Majesty?"

Doc tipped his hat. "Thank you so much. Do have a pleasant day."

She mumbled a response. He couldn't make it out, but from her expression there was no way it could have been pleasant.

Wichita, the county seat of Sedgwick County, was situated on the Arkansas River, at the mouth of the Little Arkansas, 208 miles by rail southwest of Kansas City. It was the transportation center for the abundantly rich farming region surrounding it and was an important market for broomed corn, along with slaughtering and meatpacking.

Taking leave of Doc, Raider wandered the town to stretch his legs, ending up on Broadway. So early was it, the streets were all but deserted. He stood across the street from the B & G Family Restaurant—Ladies Invited, watching the window washer attack the grimy windows with his long-poled brush. A tall and heavyset individual in a battered bowler approached, greeted the washer, unlocked the door, went inside, and turned the CLOSED sign around to OPEN.

Raider's stomach rumbled in acknowledgment of the change in sign, and he started across. Eggs, bacon, maybe sausages, hot buttered toast, and two or three cups of coffee sure would go down, sit well, and send up appreciation, he thought, if it wasn't too expensive. Paying too much for eats invariably upset his appetite. Towns the size of Wichita generally were overly expensive. He'd be damned if he'd pay more than twenty-five cents for eggs and bacon, though.

He paused upon reaching the curb and reflected a moment. Maybe he should leg it back to the station and collar Doc. Let him do the honors when the bill came.

His stomach rumbled objection. "Okay, okay, keep your shirt on."

As he expected, he was the day's first patron. The proprietor was finishing tying on his apron as he took a stool.

"How much for eggs an' bacon?"

The man tilted his head and eyed him over his spectacles. "Good morning, brother." He jerked his thumb at the price sign on the wall behind him.

"Thirty-five cents! Jesus Christ, that's highway robbery! There ain't a beanery up an' down the line for fifty mile askin' more'n twenty!"

"I can let you have week-old bread I save for the birds toasted without butter, four slices for a nickel. Can you fit that into your budget?"

"Gimme eggs an' bacon, wiseass, an' hot coffee."

"You'll have to wait on the coffee, I just turned it on."

He shuffled off through the swinging door into the kitchen. Raider could see him bent over the grill as he scraped it, hear the bacon slapped down and start to sizzle. He glanced about. The place was filthy, badly in need of painting, the floor hadn't been swept in a month, the counter desperately needed wiping, the sign announcing the prices displayed two small gobs of dried yolk, suggesting that someone had taken earlier exception to the price of eggs. The window washer outside had finished, and the window still looked dirty; the proprietor-cook picked his nose with his thumb, raised an egg, and broke it sizzling onto the grill.

Raider sighed. Homey little place, he thought, just the kind he liked. The odor of bacon crept into his nostrils.

"They soon reached the desert, where Betsy gave out,
An' down in the sand she lay rollin' about,
While Ike, half distracted, looked on with surprise,
Sayin', 'Betsy, git up, you'll git sand in your eyes.'
Singin' torral lal looral . . ."

He stopped. The man had dropped his second egg and was gaping at him.

"Smatter, don'tcha like music?"

"That's the trouble, I love music."

Raider was about to respond when the door opened, the bell at the top jingling merrily. In came two men, burly, unshaven, the shorter one bearing a hideous scar where his left eye should have been. Looking past them, Raider noted that the window washer had finished and departed. The one-eyed man stood at the door as his companion approached.

"Hey there, cookie."

"Hold your horses. Right with you."

The kitchen door swung open and the cook reappeared. The newcomer, standing behind Raider to the left, snaked his hand around Raider's back and drew Raider's .45.

"Hey, what the hell!"

"Take it easy, cowboy."

The cook stiffened, blanched, and raised his hands.

"Shake it up," called the one-eyed man.

"You heard him," said his friend. He set an empty flour sack on the counter. "Fill it up and make it fast."

"Just a—"

He fired the .45. Raider's ears rang. The slug plowed into the door behind the cook, splintering it. "Move!"

He hurried to the cash register, rang it open, and filled the sack, his hands trembling like the wings of a wounded bird. "Just opened for business. Only got—"

"You got plenty, all week's . . ."

He had sidled around the end of the counter and was checking the drawer with his free hand. Lifting it out, his eyes widened.

"Hey, looky here!"

"Don't you touch that!"

Dropping the drawer with a clatter, he began stuffing his pockets with bills. "Holding out on us, eh? Fat bastard, I oughta blow you through the wall."

"Please—"

A second shot exploded in Raider's ears, and the owner

gagged deep in his throat as if he were being strangled and slumped to the floor.

"You got something to say, cowboy?" Raider shook his head, pushing his upraised hands slightly higher. "Turn out your pockets. Everything into the bag."

Raider complied. The man leered evilly and raised the Colt.

"Somebody coming!" snapped his one-eyed companion at the door. "Let's go!"

They were gone, the bell jangling after them.

"Son of a bitch!"

The stricken proprietor had been gut-shot.

"Helllllp meeee..."

Raider ducked into the kitchen, found a wooden spoon, and clamped it between the man's teeth. Then he rushed to the door. An elderly man with a cane passed. Up the street on the other side a woman was sweeping her front stoop. There was no sign of the two holdup men. Around the corner, swinging his nightstick, came a tall, mustachioed, uniformed policeman.

"Officer! Quick!"

Doc had returned to the station after stabling the horses two blocks up the street. He glanced at his watch for the dozenth time, tried to wind it, found it already tightly wound, hissed impatiently, and marched off, following the direction Raider had taken earlier. Within minutes he found himself on Broadway at the junction of Douglas Avenue and Kellogg Street. Raider could have turned in any one of three directions, he decided. He was about to start up Kellogg when he noticed a commotion halfway down Broadway, a knot of people attracting others, including two uniformed policemen. He headed for the scene.

A towering, broad-shouldered policeman was questioning Raider, writing his answers down in a notebook. He paused every three words to lick the end of his pencil stub.

"Ain't nobody goin' to tend to poor Artemus?" snapped a woman, thrusting her hawk face between them. "He's dyin'!"

"He's done for," said Raider.

"Lucky for you he lasted long enough to get you off the hook," said the cop airily. "Now, what kind of gun were you carrying?"

"Colt forty-five. What in hell's that got to do with the price o' hen meat? Those two clowns cleaned me out proper, wallet, money, works. We stand here jawin', an' they're runnin'."

One of the two cops preceding Doc parted the crowd and inserted himself between the questioner and the woman. "What's going on, Brady?"

"Artemus Gilmore got himself shot by a holdup man."

"Rade!"

"Doc!"

"You know this man?" Brady asked Doc.

"Hell no, he just guessed my name," snapped Raider irritably.

"Let's go, fella. We can finish the questions down at the station house. All right, folks, break it up. Homer, do me a favor and call the meat wagon. I got to take this bird in."

"What in hell for?" barked Raider. "I already tol' you ever'thing that happened."

"Material witness," said Homer. "Go along with Officer Brady like a good fella."

"Do your duty as a citizen," rasped the woman.

"Mind your own goddamn business!"

"He swore at me! You heard him!" She pushed Raider; he pushed back.

Brady shoved between them. "That's enough. Come along, brother."

The drop-octagon Seth Thomas clock on the bilious green wall over the desk sergeant's head read 7:57. Extracting an Old Virginia cheroot from his new cheroot case, Doc searched his pockets for a match.

"Do you have to light up, for Chrissakes?"

The desk sergeant looked up from his newspaper. His complexion was as pink as grapefruit meat and was topped by a mop of bushy, white-blond hair. His eyebrows were even bushier. He eyed them and looked back down at his newspaper. Doc approached him.

"Do you have a match, Sergeant?" The sergeant did, and Doc lit up. "Would you have any idea how long this will take?" he asked amiably. "My partner and I were planning to catch a two-twenty train."

The sergeant cleared his throat and was about to respond when the door to his left opened and Officer Brady emerged, followed by a captain, a rugged-looking older man displaying a large, oval-shaped mole on one cheek. He appeared to be afflicted with arthritis, his body badly bent, one shoulder lower than the other and thrust forward, his right hip jutting outward, his face betraying his discomfort.

"Come in, gentlemen."

He introduced himself as Captain McCorkindale, seated them, and took his chair behind his desk, tenting his claw hands and attempting a weak and fleeting smile. The walls were cluttered with framed photographs of single officers, groups, the entire force joined by a disreputable-looking mutt. The desk was piled with papers and memorabilia, including a dirty autographed baseball sitting in a pewter ashtray.

"Mr. Rider, is it?" The captain's eyes strayed to Doc.

"Snider," said Raider. "Captain, if it's all the same to you we got to catch us a train."

"Officer Brady tells me you were the only witness to the shooting. Incidentally, I'm sorry to say Mr. Gilmore has passed on, poor soul. Didn't even make it to the hospital. So now a holdup is murder."

"I already answered all the questions."

"Appreciate your cooperation. But as I say, you're the only witness. We're going to need your testimony at the trial. You see, we know from your descriptions who these two are. Roy Beddoes and Leo Cormier. Beddoes is the one missing his eye. Where you boys staying in town?"

"We're just passing through," said Doc. "See here, Captain..."

"What's your line?"

"Beef," said Raider. "Buyin' an' sellin'."

"Mmmmm. Come to the right neck of the woods."

"Captain," began Doc, "you have Mr. Snider's answers. There's nothing he can add. Is it absolutely necessary that we hang around until you apprehend those two? It could be weeks."

"Could be never, though I doubt it will be. They specialize in restaurants and bars. They knew Mr. Gilmore kept his heavy money under the drawer. You're an eyewitness, Mr. . . ."

"Snider."

"We'll get your statement, and that'll help, no question, but you can't beat verbal testimony on the stand. They'll be sitting there like two frogs on a rock. All you'll have to do is point."

They could hear the clock outside the closed door strike nine. Raider sighed in exasperation and shifted his bulk in his chair.

"I'm sorry to inconvenience you," said the captain. "You, Mr. . . ."

"Blaisdell."

". . . I don't need. You're free to go."

"I'll stay, if you don't mind."

McCorkindale shrugged. "Would it help any if I got in touch with your home office and explained?"

"No!" rasped Raider.

His attitude was making McCorkindale begin to feel self-conscious. "Tell you what, you make out a sworn statement. Meanwhile, we've got practically every man out scouring the town. We haul them in, you finger 'em, and you can go. How's that?"

"Excellent!" snapped Doc.

Noon arrived and with it lunch provided by the taxpayers: chipped beef on soggy toast that Raider complained tasted rancid, a roll hard enough to drive nails, and tepid coffee. Doc ate nonstop and drank his coffee. Raider, having been cheated out of breakfast by the holdup, was so hungry his stomach protested vigorously and without letup. But not hungry enough to eat.

"How in hell you can put that slop into you beats me!"

"Can I have your roll?"

"Take it! Bust a damn tooth while you're at it!"

"That's not very nice."

"This is all a big joke, right? Bass an' Collins could be over the border into Mexico by now, thanks to you an' your goddamn trains. I never shoulda listened to you!"

They sat in the captain's office. He came in, greeted them warmly, shuffled through a stack of papers, found what he was looking for, and started back out.

"Sorry about the delay. It shouldn't be much longer."

"What makes you think they'll hang around town after gunnin' that poor bastard down in cold blood?" asked Raider.

The captain tapped his temple. "Hunch. Oh, say, the toilet's outside, down the hall to your left, if you need it. I'll be back. Enjoy your lunch."

The door closed.

"Fuck you, brother. What time is it?"

"Getting on to ten of one."

Neither spoke. One o'clock struck outside. One-fifteen. One-thirty. Raider paced. Doc sat.

"I gotta take a leak," said Raider. He suddenly froze in his tracks, his face brightening, beaming.

"What?"

"You come with me."

"Rade . . ."

"Just shut up an' come. We're bein' bone stupid. It's so simple I never even thought 'bout it. We go to the toilet an' climb out the window."

"Rade . . ."

"Just shut up an' come on."

"Isn't the desk sergeant going to think it's a little strange, both of us going at the same time?"

"Hell no, it could be a two-holer. If it ain't, you wait outside the door for me."

Doc sighed, shook his head, and followed him out and down to the toilet.

"This isn't going to work," he muttered.

"The hell it ain't!" He pushed through the door, took one look, and cursed vilely. Iron bars covered the window.

"Son of a bitch!"

"I knew it. This is a police station, not the Y.M.C.A."

"Get inside. Don't argue, just do it. I'm goin' back to the office. I'm countin' sixty, startin' first step I take. You count too. When you get to sixty, come back out an' head for the front door." Doc started to protest. "Just do it, goddamn it! You got us into this; I'm gettin' us out."

"*I* got us in? I didn't get involved in any holdup."

"An' I wouldn'ta had if you didn't drag us two hundred miles outta the way to this burg on the damn train. Start countin'."

Counting, Raider left him, passed the desk sergeant, nodding and smiling, and went back into the captain's office. He closed the door and rushed around the desk, pulling open the belly drawer. He found a box of matches, got the wastebasket out from under the desk and, carrying it to the door, tipped it over and set fire to the contents. Then he went back out, leaving the door slightly ajar.

Thirty-nine, forty, he counted slowly.

"Sarge?"

"What can I do for you?"

"What do you know 'bout those two clowns held up Gilmore's diner? They pretty popular round town?"

"I don't know either of them."

"You been on the force long?"

"Seven years, why?"

"Just curious. I always admire the police. Protectin' the innocent, collarin' the guilty, an' all."

"You want my autograph?"

"Would you mind?"

"Are you funning me?"

"I . . ."

The sergeant held up his hand, stopping him. He sniffed.

"Holy cow!" burst out Raider. "Look!"

Smoke came curling out of the office. The sergeant leaped to his feet and ran inside. Doc came running up. Together they raced for the front door. Just as they reached it, in came Officer Brady holding a little, ragged drunk by the collar, keeping him upright on his rubber legs. The drunk waved greeting, grinning toothlessly.

"What the . . . ?" began Brady.

"Hello," piped Doc.

"Goodbye," piped Raider.

Down the steps they bounded, heading across the street, Raider narrowly missing the extended tailgate of an empty manure wagon that was passing. A whistle blew shrilly behind them. They turned a corner, running as fast as they could, Doc in the lead, Raider puffing along behind, trying to keep up. Three blocks ahead the station platform beckoned.

"What's the time?" gasped Raider.

"About a quarter of. We've still got half an hour before the train."

"We better find someplace an' hide."

Doc swung around a corner and planted his back against a plank fence, panting, struggling to catch his breath.

"You started the place on fire."

"Oh, shit, just his damn wastebasket. Lotsa smoke, hardly any fire. It's whatcha call a diversion."

"We can't wait for the train, we've got to get out of here. Come on, let's get the horses."

He pointed up the street. Side by side they trotted to the stable. A big, heavyset young man had replaced the older man in whose care Doc had left their horses earlier.

"We want our horses," he said.

"You got 'em, Thenator, leth have your thtubth." A fat, sweaty hand opened two inches from Doc's top vest button.

"I don't have any stubs. I didn't get any."

"Tham muthta give you thtubth, thath the rule. You leave your horth, you pay, you get a thtub."

Raider pointed. "Those are our saddles, hanging side by side." He moved to get them. The man blocked him with a huge, hairy arm.

"Not till I thee your thtubth."

"Fuck the stubs!"

"I paid," insisted Doc. "We want our horses and gear."

Up the cobbled street paralleling the station platform came a fire engine, clanging loudly, the four horses in the shafts surging forward under the driver's whip. A man came running up from the opposite direction.

"Otis! Police station's on fire! Look!"

Otis came out of the doorway and with Doc and Raider looked up over the weatherbeaten sign crowning the stable. A pillar of black smoke rose straight up into the motionless air.

"Oh, for Chrissakes," moaned Raider.

"Sssssh!"

"Come on, Otis!" exclaimed the man. "Let's go see!"

"Can't, Arthur, got to mind the thtable. You go and come back and tell me."

Off ran the man.

"See here, Otis," said Doc. "As I've already told you, I wasn't given any stubs. I paid, I told him I'd be back—"

"No thtubth, no hortheth. How do I know which ith yourth? How do I know you even left any here?"

"That's my goddamn gear hanging right there in front o' your eyes!" said Raider hotly. "An' his right 'longside."

Otis flexed his shoulders and raised his sledgelike fists into fighting posture.

"You want to thtart thomething?"

"Take it easy," said Doc, gesturing placatingly.

Otis slowly lowered his fists, a triumphant grin wreathing his ugly face. Up came Raider's right, hammering him flush on the jaw. Down he went like a toppled oak, out cold.

"Let's go," said Raider. . . .

They headed south, galloping down a narrow, dusty road contiguous to the tracks, until Doc began gradually slowing. Raider followed suit. Pulling up, both looked back. The smoke pillar had grown to three times its original size and hung ominously over the city. Raider strained his ears, catching the faint sound of ringing bells.

"Sometimes I think you've got a screw loose," said Doc wearily.

"I got us the hell outta there, didn' I?"

"Oh my, yes. You just better cross your fingers and pray they don't pick up those two holdup men. They took your wallet with your I.D., remember?"

"Jesus!"

"When McCorkindale finds out your real name, Mr. Snider, and what you do for a living, he's certain to contact Chicago."

"I'm sorry, all right?"

"I know, I know. It's not you, Rade, it's me. I've just lost all heart for this nonsense."

"What nonsense? We got us a job to do."

"To you it's a job; to me it's a waste of energy." He was studying the horizon, shading the brightness from his eyes. "How far to the next town, and what is it?"

"Haysville. 'Bout ten miles down the line. I'm gonna need a gun, Doc."

"We'll find you something."

They both cast a last, rueful glance back at the smoke. On they rode side by side. Raider appraised his partner out of the corner of his eye, thought about what he'd said, and concluded he was right. He really had run out of heart for this thing. From his expression he was a million miles away, or at least a few hundred.

Back in Deadwood with his Lydia-Mae.

CHAPTER SIX

Looking for a needle in a haystack paled by comparison with looking for Sam Bass and Joel Collins in Texas. Stretching from the Sabine and Red rivers in the east to the Rio Grande in the west, the Lone Star State covered exactly 267,339 square miles. Boarding the Chicago, Rock Island & Pacific in Mulvane over Raider's strenuous objections, they crossed over into Oklahoma and by sundown the following day had wheeled the territory behind them and entered Texas, pulling into Ringgold and the junction of the Chicago, Rock Island & Pacific and Missouri, Kansas & Texas Railway.

Raider stood on the station platform mumbling his by now all but patented diatribe against travel by rail and examining his newly purchased secondhand Peacemaker.

"This thing's a buncha junk," he observed.

"What do you want for four dollars, a hand-tooled Gatling gun?"

A man rolled an overloaded baggage cart by them. A suitcase poised perilously at the top of the pile slipped, dropped, and landed with a thud a scant inch from Raider's foot.

"Whyncha watch what the hell you're doin'?" he burst out angrily.

"Whyncha get outta the goddamn way!" responded the man.

Doc grabbed Raider's arm and walked him off. A lovely

brunette with a bird on her hat, a flawless complexion, and the loveliest, most seductive lips Doc had ever seen passed them, batting her eyes invitingly at him. To Raider's surprise he limited his response to a forced smile and a gallant, if uninspired, tip of his hat.

"You can't really blame that fire on me," whined Raider, ignoring the lady.

"Who started it?"

"That dumb desk sergeant shoulda put it out. He musta panicked, got his legs tangled up, an' kicked the damn basket all over the office. Why we stoppin' here, anyways?"

"This is Texas."

"Big deal. What's the plan, buttonhole folks an' ask if they've seen Mr. Fish an' his friend? Then move on to the next town? Christ Almighty, we'll have beards down to our knees by the time we get to Dallas."

"Let's go find the law. On second thought, you see to the horses, I'll find the law. And relax, the one thing in our favor is the fact that Bass and Collins have been busy. I'll bet the wires have been humming from Scotts Bluff to Galveston."

"Jesus Christ, not that far down."

"Before we go any further, we, you and I, have to make a pact. Promise each other we'll both stay clear of trouble— anything that might delay us further. Promise?"

"Doc, trouble ain't like a damn snake, it don't rattle warnin'."

"Please, do the best you can. And, oh yes, if the stableman gives stubs, be sure you get them. And don't lose them. We don't need a repeat of Wichita."

Off he sailed, leaving Raider holding the reins of the grulla mustang and Doc's big bay stallion. Ringgold impressed Doc as only slightly tidier than Deadwood. At least it could lay claim to a peace officer, although the man behind the marshal's badge who rose from his quarter-sawed, halfback rocking chair to greet him looked somewhat less than impressive. He had no chin. That is, if he had one, so far back in his face was it that it was all but absent. Noticing this upon entering, it crossed Doc's mind that having no chin had its advantages. For one thing, it deprived an adversary of perhaps the most inviting place to strike a blow. Marshall Ewart B. Bonds affected spectacles, which could also—at least conceivably—give an attacker pause. His eyes behind the lenses were enormous, suggesting great magnification.

He was in his mid-forties, lean, lazy-looking, with a prominent pivot tooth dominating his uppers, overhanging the space that should have been occupied by his lower jaw. His nose appeared to be clogged; it rattled wetly when he spoke, and droplets of mucus occasionally shot forth, landing on his knees.

Doc introduced himself, flashed his I.D. card, and explained his mission.

"Sam Bass and Joel Collins. Robbed the U.P. office in Big Spring, didn't they?" asked Bonds.

"A while back. My partner and I have reason to believe they've come back down here."

"I got no new wanted dodgers on either one. How about we look at the paper."

He rose, beckoned, and walked Doc to the back room, where three cells—all unoccupied—were located. Dead flies filled the sills of the barred windows. A four-drawer file cabinet leaned against the wall in one corner, the top drawer half opened and crammed with papers. A stack of newspapers half the height of the cabinet were piled against it. The sun slanting through the dusty glass of the single window facing a lot in the rear illuminated a single live dung fly. It wandered up, then back down the sill, as if to assure itself of privacy. Coming to rest, its forelegs poised, it rubbed them together like a moneylender displaying his greed. It basked briefly in the warmth, then flew over to the file cabinet.

"I got *Montague County Intelligencer*s back to last year. Today's is right on top. Help yourself."

Doc began leafing through the paper. No news from Wichita, he was relieved to see. Elated better described his reaction when he came to the back page and glanced over it.

BASS AND COLLINS STEAL AGAIN

Word has been received in Montague that those well-known flouters of law and order, Sam Bass and partner, Joel Collins, are back in Texas and rampaging again. They have hit the Wells Fargo Bank here for the tidy sum of $18,000. Sheriff Matt Gorsline, having alerted his fellow peace officers up and down the line, has organized a posse and is giving chase to the holdup men. His Honor, our esteemed mayor, is offering a $1,000 reward for information leading to the arrest and conviction of Bass and Collins.

Readers will recall that the same pair appropriated close to $78,000 in a holdup of the Union Pacific office in Big Spring some time back.

Marshal Bonds was back in his chair, his feet up on his desk, rolling a cigarette when Doc came back with the newspaper.

"Pay dirt," he said. "They showed up in Montague."

"That close by, eh? You're in luck."

"Maybe. This paper's dated two days ago. By now they could be all the way to El Paso."

"Maybe not, not with the pickin's good as they are round these parts." Bonds lowered his feet, moistened his cigarette, lit up, and puffed. "'Sides, they got a passal o' friends down Denton County way—hop, skip, an' a jump from here, roun' Hickory Creek, in Gorza an' Lewisville."

"You seem to know quite a bit about them."

"Know 'bout Bass. He was a busy bee back in his Denton County days. Pop'lar fella."

"How far to Montague?"

"How far can you spit? Half hour at a trot."

"You've been very helpful, Marshal, I appreciate it."

"Hell, I ain't done a thing. Didn't even see the piece in the paper. Good huntin', only mind you watch your hat. They say Collins can fill a bird's backside at two hunnerd yards."

• • •

Doc waited for Raider in front of the Ringgold Saloon across the street from the marshal's office, watching to near distraction farm wagons and buggies, freight wagons and cowhands on horseback pass back and forth. But there was no sign of Raider. It was suffocatingly hot, he was tired, thirsty, hungry, and suddenly on fire to get to Montague, hopefully onto the outlaws' track, and wind the thing up.

Then what? Maybe go back to Deadwood and put some fresh flowers on her grave. A long trip for such a gesture. But a meaningful gesture. On second thought, why bother? She wasn't really buried there. Not for a moment; her grave was in his heart. It was a heavy burden and one he fancied he would be carrying to his own grave. Apart from losing her, the tragedy had soured his taste for the chase, for action, danger, and guns. Had flushed it out of his system. Finish this business and it would be goodbye, Pinkerton National Detective Agency. Goodbye, Rade.

He was preparing to go looking for Raider when who should wander by, twirling her parasol, the bird on her hat looking so real he half expected it to take off, her lovely green eyes filling with him, her crimson mouth gleaming seductively, but the brunette he had seen on the station platform.

He doffed his hat.

"Good morning."

She stood twirling, one hip thrust forward, her black silk dress trimmed with white lace gleaming like a grackle's back.

"My name's Adelaide."

"I'm . . . Mr. Nothing. George Nothing."

"What?"

"I'm sorry, I don't mean to be rude. Any other time, place . . . Forgive me, I'm . . . just not interested."

She stared and twirled and clucked softly. *"Tsk, tsk,* what a pity."

A sudden commotion erupted inside the saloon behind him. A man built along the lines of a Shorthorn steer came staggering out, cupping his eye with his hand and muttering

curses. He found momentary support against the post brac-
ing the overhang and caught his breath. Then, shaking off
the blow, he wheeled and started back inside. The unmis-
takable sound of fist encountering bone to the accompani-
ment of foul language was suddenly audible. Doc thought
he recognized one of the cursers. Instinct goaded by suspicion impelled him to investigate.

His heart sank at what he saw. Ringed by their audience,
the returning patron and Raider stood toe to toe, flailing
away. The big one stood a full head taller than Raider and
outweighed him by forty or fifty pounds, but he was slow
of fist and even slower of foot. Raider landed a crushing
one-two, doubling him over, and was preparing to finish
him off when the bartender raised a bottle high and brought
it down squarely on his head. Raider stiffened and collapsed
in a groaning heap. The onlookers cheered and applauded.

Doc got him up on his feet and herded him outside and
down the steps to the horse trough. He ducked him once,
bringing him up sputtering. Raider shook it off and glared
viciously. Parasol and lady were nowhere about.

"Rade . . ."

"Don't start, Doc. Don't say nothin'. It wasn't my fault."

"It never is. What did you do, try and start a fire in the
wastebasket?"

Raider didn't seem to hear him. He was concentrating
on gingerly investigating the spot where the bottle had landed
and checking the tips of his fingers for blood.

"What hit me?"

"What shatters? You're lucky he didn't use a ball bat."

"Do you know what that overgrowed son of a bitch said,
that big bastard with the cornsilk hair an' the glass jaw? He
said anybody from Arkansas fucks razorbacks, that it's a
knowed fact an' recognized far an' wide as the most pop'lar
sport in the entire state, that even Governor Bill Miller does
it. On the damn State House lawn! That's an insult, Doc."

"It sounds like one, but is it enough to start a war over?
Everybody's staring. Let's go. Where are the horses?"

"Up the street."

They walked, Raider continuing to feel his head and explore his teeth with his fingers to reassure himself that the total he now had coincided with that prior to hostilities. Doc got him off the subject of his home state and onto Bass and Collins and Montague.

"It's beautiful, Rade, a gift from heaven. Our first real break in the case."

"Yeah, only a little bit stale. To tell you the honest truth, at the moment I don't muchly give a shit 'bout Montague. I'm too damn hungry. I'm about to keel over. Can't we eat before we run?"

They ate, downing thick sirloin steaks awash in gravy, potatoes, freshly baked hot berry pie, and coffee. They were seated at a window table, and throughout the meal Doc rarely took his eyes from the street. He stared out, surveying it from end to end.

"You lookin' for that little round-ass gal with the fancy hat an' the umbrella?"

"Parasol. Not really. The last thing I need is a woman, any woman, even the prettiest in the land. Too much on my mind, I guess."

"Get yourself a woman an' she'll get it off your mind. You know, hair o' the dog that bit you."

"You have a marvelous way with words, Rade, but no thanks."

They finished eating, Doc paid the bill, and they headed for the stable. Marshal Ewart B. Bonds, sporting a Buntline Special, sixteen-inch barrel and all, greeted them in businesslike fashion.

"You, buckaroo," he said, addressing Raider. "'Fraid you're gonna have to come along with me."

"What in hell for? Who is this guy, Doc?"

"He appears to be wearing a badge," responded Doc dryly. "What's up, Marshal?"

"Got to cage your friend here. On complaint o' Lassiter Tibbs, the town punchin' bag. He seems to be missin' a couple front teeth, an' his nose is busted for fair. He claims courtesy o' your fists, buckaroo."

"He started it, an' kindly stop callin' me fuckin' buck-aroo!"

"Come along, please. Don't make no scene. I don't wanna have to bring you in at gunpoint in front o' all these nice folks."

"All right, all right."

Doc threw up his hands, shook his head, and followed them.

CHAPTER SEVEN

Fate appeared to be playing her little shell game with Raider and Doc, showing them the pea, covering, switching, exposing the empty shell. Bass and Collins were the pea; the shells were locales; the delays, like the present one, were destiny's monkey wrenches, coming thick and fast, denying them the satisfaction of finding the pea.

Doc sat on one side of the bars, Raider the other, his ire up, his face red-to-purple, his eyes fired and flaming.

"This is bullshit! Pure an' simple!"

"For the tenth time, take it easy. The man is the law here in Ringgold."

"The man is a ring-tailed asshole!"

"Ssssh, he can hear you. Don't make things any worse than they are."

"If a son of a bitch insulted your home state o' Massachusetts, wouldn't it get your dander up? Wouldn't it?"

"Oh my, yes. I'd probably beat him to death!"

"Right. How long you figger I'll be cooped up in here?"

"Until the trial and the hanging. How do I know? Bonds is calling the turn. Every peace officer in every town writes his own rule book. You should know that by now. Just sit here and relax. Meanwhile, I'll take a run over to Montague and see what I can find on our friends."

"What do you wanna do that for? Why can'tcha wait for me?"

Doc stood up, smoothing his vest, then respositioning his derby. "I may not live that long."

"You're funny, you know that, Weatherbee? Funnier than the cow with four broke legs."

The relative quiet that pervaded Ringgold gradually gave way to a muted din as the shadows lengthened, the sun set, and evening descended upon the town. A gun went off. Raider, standing at the window, scowled. People could shoot off guns, risk life and limb, and likely get a pat on the back from the marshal. But let an outsider defend the honor of his home state against some loudmouth's insults and he gets bars and beans.

The door opened and in came Bonds, carrying a tray with a plate of steaming beans, bread, and a tin cup of coffee.

"Chow time."

Raider grunted.

"Aren't you hungry?"

"How long you gonna keep me cooped up here?"

"He swore out a complaint. He's got witnesses. Judge'll be showin' up tomorrow mornin'. He'll hear both sides, likely fine you ten dollars for disturbin' the peace, maybe a buck for each o' the teeth you knocked out." Another shot rang out outside, followed by a heart-rending scream and two more shots. "An' turn you loose."

"Tomorrow."

"That's good news, ain't it?"

Again Raider grunted. The marshal unlocked the door and handed him his tray.

"I gotta bottle o' Ruckus Juice out front. Care for a jolt?"

"Rather have the whole bottle."

Bonds eyed him sympathetically. "I'm plumb sorry 'bout this, buckaroo, but brawlin' an' bustin' is disturbin' the peace."

"May be, but if that overgrowed asshole hadn'ta swore out the complaint you wouldn'ta done nothin', wouldja?"

"Nope."

"Goddamn it!"

"Don't go gettin' your feathers back up."

"It's not that, it's this." He gestured, taking in the confines of his cell. "It's knowin' that I coulda just as well beat his head off an' still only have to pay the damn ten dollars."

Arriving in Montague, Doc discovered the sheriff's office was locked. According to the newspaper, Sheriff Gorsline was out hunting Bass and Collins, and he was probably still doing so. It was the middle of the afternoon. Doc repaired to the Full-Drop Spur Saloon, the handiest watering hole, commandeered a table, and ordered a glass of Martingale's Imported 100-proof Scotch Whiskey: "The Taste of the Highlands." The waiter set a bottle of ominously dark-looking Taos Lightning on the table, wiped his nose with the back of his hand, and frowned intimidatingly.

"This here's the closest we got to Martingale's, imported from New Mexico."

"It'll do, thank you," said Doc diplomatically.

He poured half a tumblerful and tasted it warily. In an instant the tip of his tongue felt as if it had been bitten. It was on fire with pain!

"Water!" he roared, jumping up, upsetting table and chair. "Water! Water!" Grabbing his throat with both hands, he began dancing a spirited jig, prompting two of his nearest neighbors to begin clapping their hands and stomping their feet in rhythm. The waiter rushed over with a pitcher of water, dashing him in the face. The stompers bellowed laughter.

"Towel," said Doc quietly.

Marshal Bonds came in to say good night to his solitary prisoner. He found him lying on his cot, staring at the ceiling, talking to himself, continuing to fume over his predicament.

"It's nine o'clock. I'm closin' up for the night. Need anythin' afore I go?"

"You might let me borrow the damn key."

"Be back seven o'clock or thereabouts. Bring you a nice hot breakfast."

"Bring me that judge you mentioned. Better him than biscuits."

"Patience, buckaroo. G'night."

He left. Raider could hear the outside door close and the key turn in the lock. He got up and, gripping the bars, tested them. They were solid steel; so well constructed was the door it barely jiggled. The window bars were likewise set in Portland cement. He sat down on his cot, picked up the tin cup, and hurled it against the wall.

"Son of a bitch!"

Time passed on mud-slowed feet. The din of Ringgold's night life increased in volume. Everybody in the world seemed to be having a great old time, and here he sat, stuck like a coon in a double-spring Newhouse trap.

"Son of a bitch!"

He started, listening. Somebody was outside the door. The lock shattered as they broke in, slamming the door against the office wall. Then closing it. Heavy steps approached. The inner door opened. There stood Lassiter Tibbs, his smile framing his missing front tooth.

"Well, looky here, if it ain't the razorback fucker hisself."

"What in hell do you want? Come by to gloat? Whatta ya mean, bustin' in here? I heard. Breaking down official doors is 'gainst the law, you know. You could go to jail."

"Not in this here town. Not with Uncle Ewart on the job."

"Uncle?"

"You don't like it inside there?"

"I love it. See for yourself—all the comforts o' home."

"You don't like it, why don't we let you out?"

"Wait a minute."

"Philander Will!"

What sounded like a bull stomping just before the charge stiffened Raider. He gaped and swallowed. A shadow fell across the floor. Filling the doorway was the biggest man he had ever seen. Perhaps not the tallest, perhaps not the widest, perhaps not the biggest chest, or the most muscular, but without question the most impressive combination of the four. So huge he couldn't make it through the door walking forward, but had to turn sideways, duck his massive head, and sidle through. Straightening, he grinned at Lassiter.

"Arkansaw, this here's my little brother, Philander Will. Say hello to the man, Philander Will."

"'Lo."

Again Raider swallowed. "Jesus Christ, what a monster."

"Time's a-wastin'," said Lassiter, rubbing his hands together and showing his gap. "Let's get you outta there. Philander Will, fetch us the key ring from outside."

Philander Will nodded, reached around the jamb, and held up the key ring.

"Give it here. I'll do the honors."

"Hold ever'thin'!" protested Raider. "You can't do this. I'm not goin' anyplace."

Lassiter shook his head, his grin firmly, permanently stamped on his face. "You're comin' with us."

He inserted the proper key. Raider's hand shot through the bars, grabbed the ring, and jerked it free. Then he flung it behind him.

"That's that, shitkicker, now get the hell outta here, both o' you! Beat it!"

"You shouldna done that. 'Twarn't fair. You're comin' with us!"

"Not now."

Raider laughed brittlely. Lassiter nodded to Philander Will and stepped aside. Philander Will approached the cell door, gripped the bars, and shook them.

"Good luck!" said Raider. "That's Pittsburgh steel. Solid as hell's anchor."

"Go 'head, Philander Will. Don't stand on ceremony, boy."

Raider's eyes widened. He backed away. Philander Will tightened his grip, pulled again, was unable to budge the bars, released them, backed off four steps, lowered his shoulder, backed off two more steps, and came barreling forward. Once, twice, three times, he crashed against the bars, releasing tiny puffs of cement powder from the upright braces on either side.

"You quit that, you son of a bitch! Right now!"

Ignoring him, Philander Will changed shoulders and charged again. The upper hinge and the lock snapped simultaneously. Raider gasped and gaped. Seizing the door, the giant pulled it loose and flung it to one side like a wooden gate.

"You comin' out or are we comin' in to get you?" asked Lassiter.

Sheriff Matt Gorsline was old. Sitting across from him in his office, Doc put him at eighty, possibly eighty-five. His hair and beard were past white, into yellow. The visible portions of his face were deeply lined. His eyes were rheumy. His lips were dried and shrunken against his mouth. He looked to be weary of life, of the job and responsibilities it entailed. Doc could not even picture him exerting the effort required to mount a horse. But evidently he was able to, having just come in from six solid hours of chasing.

"What gripes me is that two days back one o' the boys spotted them. Swears he did. Down around Sunset, not two hours after they hit the Wells Fargo bank here in town."

"I gather you think they're long gone now."

Gorsline nodded, jerked open the bottom drawer of his desk, produced two tumblers and a half-bottle of bourbon. He poured. They drank. It bit, but nothing like the Taos Lightning he'd been bitten by earlier, reflected Doc. He made a mental note never to yell for water again when a liquid rattlesnake struck his tongue.

"Any ideas where they might be heading?"

Gorsline pondered the question a long moment before shaking his head. "Only away from these parts. Which just stands to reason. I don't have anything in the way of information."

"You must have a hunch."

"If I followed hunches they'd have taken away my tin a

hundred years ago." He studied Doc out from under his pink upper lids. "Course a man's entitled to his private, personal hunches."

"Where?"

"Big Spring."

"They've already been there. Seems to me that'd be the last place they'd head."

"Would seem so to a lot of people. Which might be a good excuse to go back."

"I don't know, Sheriff. It's a long ride for what could be a wild goose chase."

"I can't argue that." Gorsline held his palms out to his side in a gesture of helplessness. Doc read it correctly. He nodded and stood up.

"Finish your drink, why don't you?"

Doc obliged him. "I've got to get back."

"Sorry I can't help. Mister, I sure do hate this time, after the chase, coming home empty, beat to boots and neck deep in disappointment, failure. Makes a man feel like he's getting old."

"I know the feeling."

"Real old. Old as the hills. The pity of it is I won't even hit sixty-five till the day before Christmas."

Doc hammered the door as hard as he could. "Marshal, it's me! Open up!"

Bonds appeared, his hair mussed, his eyes bleary, yawning.

"You. What time is it?"

"Never mind. They've broken into your jail and kidnapped my partner!"

"Oh, bullshit."

The door started to close. Doc shoved his foot in it, then pushed it wide.

"Get dressed. It must have been that kid who filed the complaint and his pals. Is he dangerous? Raider's in the soup, isn't he? Isn't he?"

"Calm down. If it was Lassiter busted in he's in no

danger. On the other hand, if it was his little brother..."

"The front door was broken and the cell door ripped from its hinges."

"My, my. That'd be Philander Will. Him, he's dangerous. I've seen him bulldog a full-growed steer, bust its neck bare armed. He's big as a corn crib an' strong as any two strongmen you've ever seen, I mean put together."

"Get dressed, hurry!"

Bonds yawned and excused himself. "Can't it wait till daylight?"

"No! Move!"

Lassiter lit the fourth lamp and set it on the bare ground, defining the ring. Philander Will had stripped to the waist. He stood opposite Raider, flexing his incredible arms, shadowboxing, and smirking at the Pinkerton. About twenty men had gathered to watch the festivities.

What festivities? mused Raider, watching Philander Will aghast. He wasn't about to fight the bastard, not for a minute. Not for two seconds. One blow from either of the anvils at the ends of his wrists would break him in half, shatter his skull, fill his head flesh with a hundred fragments of bone. No, thank you!

The night air was surprisingly cool, he thought. Or was it just his nerves? Everybody in view seemed to be sweating. He was himself, icy droplets deserting his armpits, running down his rib cage, beading his brow, his cheeks, his upper lip. The moon was full and focused on Lassiter's ring. The crowd was passing two bottles around, warming up for the entertainment. For the slaughter. Visualizing his imminent destruction in his mind's eye, Raider began feeling all the old aches and pains from the injuries incurred in his fracas with Doc. In ten seconds he was hurting all over. And the gunshot wound he'd suffered in the shoot-out earlier began acting up something fierce.

"Take off your shirt, Arkansaw," blurted Lassiter.

"Fuck you, Buster. You wanna see a fight, you fight him. Count this ol' boy out."

"We're countin' you in. Right, Philander Will?"

"Right, Lassie."

Philander Will continued shadowboxing. He looked to be twice as fast as his brother, noted Raider, and surprisingly nimble on his feet for three hundred or so pounds. He had to weigh that much easily. He stood close to six-eight and outreached him by a good six inches. Damned if he'd be a willing participant in his own murder! Where the hell were they? he wondered. How far from town, from Uncle Ewart? Uncle or no, he'd put a stop to this farce. He would if he could.

"Take off your shirt," repeated Lassiter.

"Go to hell."

Lassiter came at him, grabbing fistfuls of his shirt. Raider pushed him off.

"All right, all right, all right. No need to rip the goddamn thing!" He undid his shirt and removed it, feeling a dull flash of pain in his wounded shoulder as he raised his arm.

Lassiter cackled. "You look like you been through a Comanche gauntlet. Whatta mess. 'Nother lick here or there nobody'll notice, right? Let's go. Who's got the tin?"

"Here she be," piped a voice.

He was handed a pie tin and a wooden spoon. He took up his stance in the center of the ring.

"Okay, boys, come here to me an' I'll give you your 'structions."

Philander Will approached him. Raider stood rooted in his corner.

"I can hear from over here."

"Okay, Arkansaw. By the way, you gotta name?"

"Killer. Killer O'Toole, former state o' Arkansas heavyweight champeen o' the world."

Philander Will chortled exultantly and held up one of his anvils.

"Former's right," said Lassiter. "Okay, listen close. When I bang the tin, that starts a roun'. When little brother knocks you down, that ends the roun'. When I bangs the tin, that starts the nex' roun'. When little brother knocks you down, that ends the roun'. When I bangs . . ."

"All right, all right. Jesus Christ, you're as blow-mouthed borin' as you are big."

"May the best man win!"

The response to this was a chorus of raucous laughter, energetic knee slapping, elbowing, and applause. Raider didn't think it all that funny. Lassiter banged the pie tin and backed off. Philander Will came out of his corner waving his anvils. Raider stood rooted.

"Come on, Killer. Come out an' fight like a man!" said Lassiter.

"Like hell. I got no beef with him. You wanna fight, I'll fight you. Or are you yellow?"

The man who had handed Lassiter the tin spoke up. "Lassie can't fight you. He's a-hurtin'. He was hurted in a fight."

More laughter. Lassiter's eyes narrowed.

"You comin' out or you want him to come in there an' get you?"

Philander Will needed no second invitation. He came barreling at Raider, who promptly sidestepped him. Philander Will turned and came back, circling slowly, deliberately. He swung. Raider pulled clear, feeling the breeze from the blow. Again and again the big man swung, missed, grit his teeth, deepened his scowl, and struck again.

"Fight him, Killer! Stand your ground an' swing, yaller bastard!"

Raider danced away, ducked, sidestepped, and otherwise evaded blow after blow. Until Philander Will abruptly altered the attack, lowering his huge head, surging forward, and ramming Raider full in the chest. He bounced as he hit the ground. Every rib in his cage was shattered, he thought. Pain flooded his chest. He was afraid to look down lest he see his heart, crushed by the blow, spurting blood through his flesh.

Philander Will had backed off and was readying himself for a second rush. Raider rolled over, sprang up on hands and knees, shook off the pain and threatening dizziness, and lurched to his feet.

"That's more like it!" roared Lassiter. "We finally got us a fight here, boys."

Again Philander Will attacked. This time Raider managed to dodge him. This success imbued him with false courage, leading to a disastrous mistake. As the big man passed by, he shot a right, catching him flush on the temple. It knocked him off balance, but he managed to keep his feet. Stopped, he turned slowly, his expression murderous.

"You hit me."

"Sorry," said Raider, holding his hands up defensively. "I lost my head for a sec there."

"You hurt."

"Sorry, damn it!"

Philander Will sprang at him, swinging wildly. Raider took a hard shot to his shoulder wound and one to his shattered ribs. They *were* shattered—had to be. Mere bone can't possibly stand a blow from a battering ram. He had heard no telltale cracking sound, but the pain was indescribable. And the blow following up only intensified it. Philander Will swam before his eyes. Why fight it? Why not collapse, faint dead away?

"Jesus Christ, no," he muttered. "I pass out an' the son of a bitch'll stomp me to death. If he doesn't, his brother will!"

His legs felt like rolled-up towels, his heart pounded furiously, sweat poured down into his eyes, blinding him. The salt stung and burned. He backed away. Philander Will came at him, swinging wildly, tirelessly. One more hit.

A gun cracked. Two more shots. Philander Will froze. Everyone did, the scene suddenly resembling a woodcut. Then the onlookers parted and Marshal Bonds, his smoking Buntline in hand, came forward followed by Doc. Raider recognized them and tried to smile relief, then rolled his eyes up in their sockets, dropped to his knees, and fell over on his face, out cold.

The last sound he heard was the beating of the pie tin and Lassiter shouting, "End o' roun' one. Roun' two comin' up!"

CHAPTER EIGHT

Raider's ribs were not broken, although their bending and bruising rewarded him with, in his opinion, as much pain as if they'd been "busted proper." Fortunately, he emerged from the fray little the worse for Philander Will's manhandling, and it was Doc's view that his passing out had to be precipitated by fear rather than pain of injury.

Unfortunately for both, the situation was to take on an unforeseeable bad turn in spite of the marshal's well-timed interruption. The five of them—Bonds, the Tibbs brothers, Raider, and Doc—stood in the lawman's office listening to him explain the situation.

"You, Lassiter an' Philander Will, I'm jailin' on charges o' disturbin' the peace an' stagin' a bare-knuckle prizefight, which both o' you know is illegal in Montague County."

Raider applauded. Doc stopped him.

"You, buckaroo, I'm jailin' for engagin' in same."

Raider exploded. "Those two sons o' bitches forced me! Snatched me outta my cell, took me to an ol' barn that stunk worse'n perdition, kep' me stewin' an' frettin' for hours, then forced me to fight! Fight or get killed!"

"Okay, okay, I'll drop the charge o' engagin' in same."

"That's better."

"But there's still the matter o' breakin' jail."

"I didn' break nothin', damn it, don't you listen? Man Mountain Mushface there ripped off the door, an' they forced me—"

"Okay, okay, I'll drop the charge o' jail breakin'."

"Breakin' is right!"

"Excuse me, Marshal," interposed Doc. "While you're at it, I think it would be in everyone's best interests if you also dropped the original charge."

"I can't do that."

"The hell you can't, Uncle!" burst out Raider.

"Marshal, my partner was originally charged on this man's complaint. Now he's filing a charge of his own against both of them, Lassiter for abduction, Philander Will for assault and battery. Okay, we'll agree to drop both charges if Lassiter'll drop his. Two for one."

"That ain't fair!" barked Raider.

"Shut up, Rade."

"You a lawyer?" asked the marshal. "You should be; you talk pretty like one. Okay, only what 'bout my busted door?"

"I'm sure these gentlemen will be happy to restore it. The expense should be paltry, inconsequential. A small price for their freedom."

Doc eyed one Tibbs, then the other. Philander Will continued to grin. Whether he was enjoying the bargaining, reflecting on his triumph, or physically incapable of altering his expression Doc could not decide. The deal was done; Raider and he moved off. By now it was nearing midnight. They took a room only slightly larger than a broom closet— the only one available in the Ringgold Hotel—and retired for the night.

Doc's first idea of the new day made sense to Raider, marking one of the historic occasions when a strategy suggested by his partner met with his approval. Rather than chase about Texas in quest of their quarry they would head straight for the nearest sizable town and consult the local newspaper, on the theory that Bass and Collins's crimes would betray their whereabouts.

The nearest town of size turned out to be Fort Worth, approximately ninety miles south-southwest of Ringgold. Before leaving town, at Doc's insistence they would take time to wire Chicago in order to update the home office on their activities.

The clerk on duty at the Western Union office bore a vague resemblance to Marshal Bonds, prompting Raider to remark offhandedly that everybody in town seemed to be related to everybody else. The clerk, engrossed in repairing his telegraph key, overheard him.

"You talkin' 'bout Cousin Ewart? Oh say, 'scuse my bad manners, I'll be right with you boys."

He finished screwing the key assembly securely in place and came over to the counter.

"We'd like to send a wire to Chicago. To the home office of the Hercules Plow and Harvester Company," said Doc.

"Hercu . . . Say, either o' you go by the name o' Blaisdell?"

"I'm Martin Blaisdell," said Doc.

"Martin, that's the name. I got a message for you."

"How come you didn't deliver it?" asked Raider, squinting at him suspiciously.

"I was jus' 'bout to call my nephew over to go lookin' for you. It just came in not ten minutes ago." He held up one finger, requesting patience, and began going through a file drawer. "Blasidell, Blaisdell, Blaisdell. Here we be."

Doc waited until they were outside before opening the envelope.

"Mr. Storm," grumbled Raider.

"Let's hope, and not Mr. Flood."

"Flood suits me."

Doc shook the message down to one end of the envelope and tore off the other.

NO PROGRESS REPORT FORTHCOMING YOU MANY DAYS STOP
WHAT IS CURRENT STATUS OF TWO PRIZE ACCOUNTS STOP ARE
SAME LANDED STOP IF NOT WHY NOT STOP INFORMATION RE-
CEIVED THIS OFFICE SUGGESTING POSSIBILITIES IN NAZINOTY
STOP POSSIBLY UNFOUNDED RUMOR STOP SUGGEST YOU CHECK
STOP REPORT REPORT REPORT

"What's Naz—"
"Code, Rade, let me check the book."

They withdrew into the privacy of a nearby alley. Doc got out his code book.

"What does it mean?"

"Ssssh, give me a chance. H...u...t..."

"Hutchins!"

"Texas?"

"You betcha."

Doc sucked in his breath and held it. And screwed up his face as if expecting to be stabbed. "How far?"

"Hop, skip, an' a jump. Little ways past Dallas. Jus' the other side. No more than a hundred and thirty miles or so."

"A—"

"Easy, easy. This is Texas, Doc. A hundred and thirty Texas miles is a Sunday afternoon stroll, for Chrissakes."

Doc was preparing to respond when they heard footsteps. They had withdrawn about twenty feet into the alley. The lady with the parasol, same dress, same beauty, different hat passed. She glanced at them. Doc touched the brim of his hat in greeting.

"Good morning."

She turned her face forward, saying nothing, her expression unaltered in the slightest. She walked on, vanishing from sight.

"Good mornin' to you, Weatherbee. You sure ain't lost the ol' charm!"

Philander Will had not broken Raider, but he had hurt him. Had filled his bag with pain that became more pronounced when he tried to mount his horse.

"I can do it! I can do it!" he barked in frustration, gritting his teeth.

"You know you can't. If you can't even mount, you certainly can't ride."

Doc dismounted, grabbed Raider by the back of his belt, and pulled him to the ground before he could throw his leg over.

"We'll take the train."

"Like hell!"

They were standing out front of the stable in the bright,

early morning sunshine, pedestrians and traffic passing them.
Two prune-visaged old maids, gliding by, heard Raider swear,
pursed their wrinkled lips, and destroyed him with their
eyes.

"Keep your voice down."

"Please, Doc. Them sudden stops an' starts like to snap
my spine. Fair's fair. I give in to you comin' down from
Scotts Bluff. You got to give in now."

"You can't sit a horse; you won't ride the train. What
about the stage?"

Raider brightened. "That'll do fine."

"All that jolting and jouncing?"

"It beats the train six ways from breakfast."

Doc checked his watch. "It's almost seven-thirty. Let's
get the horses over to the train depot and make arrangements
to ship them. Then grab the first stage out."

Doc had long nursed a theory regarding his partner's
ingrained dislike of the iron horse. So enamored was Raider
of the real thing—of flesh, blood, mane, and saddle—he
could not abide alternative transport. But riding the stage
at least put him in proximity to horseflesh, representing the
next best thing. Having, during his career, suffered many
an injury that made it impossible for him to ride a horse,
he had logged thousands of miles in Concord coaches.

He admired the sturdiness of the vehicle, its imaginative
design, in particular the suspension of the carriage on two
thoroughbraces, three-inch-thick leather straps that served
as shock absorbers. The rocking motion imparted by this
arrangement bothered some passengers, but to him the
thoroughbraces made the coach a cradle on wheels.

At eight o'clock the southbound stage from Wichita Falls
pulled into the depot. The team of six well-dusted trotters,
in loosened harness, fly-flicked their tails, bobbed their
noble heads, and stomped, impatient to move on. The stage
was loaded. Leather pouches fat with mail were crammed
into the front boot, beneath the driver's seat. On top of them
went the iron strongbox containing valuables. Bags of newspapers and magazines and express packages were stowed

in a second, larger boot at the rear. Passenger baggage also found its way into the rear boot as well as on top and inside.

Eight passengers, one less than the full inside complement, including the two Pinkertons, climbed through the door. Each one's ticket guaranteed him a space only about fifteen inches wide on the upholstered seats. They sat knee to knee, Raider taking the best seat available, the one back to the driver. The driver climbed up on his box, the messenger, double-barreled shotgun in hand, climbed up alongside him, the driver bawled, the reins snapped, the coach lurched, and off they rolled.

Doc sat opposite Raider. A well- and expensively dressed young man sat between them on the center bench. His only means of support was the leather loop suspended from the ceiling over his head. Leaving Ringgold, taking the road down to Montague, the going was fairly level, imparting a soothing, almost lulling motion to the coach. The young man between Raider and Doc introduced himself.

"Cuthbertson's the name, the law's my game."

Adroitly flicking his business card from his breast pocket, he presented it to Raider, who eyed it disdainfully and grunted. Undaunted, Lawyer Cuthbertson pivoted and proferred the card to Doc, who politely accepted it.

"I'm Martin Blaisdell. This is my associate, Mr. O'Toole. We're in farm machinery."

"You're in a Concord coach at the moment," snapped Cuthbertson, punctuating this sally with a nerve-piercing laugh, thin, high-pitched, and alarmingly grating. It sounded to Raider like a length of barbed wire being jerked through a fence. A hundred and thirty miles of it, he reflected, and either he'd jump out the window or toss Mr. Flasharity Lawbooks through it.

Again Cuthbertson laughed. At nothing.

"What are you doin'?" asked Raider. "Tunin' up?"

From his expression in reaction the lawyer did not understand, but nevertheless accorded him a friendly smile.

"Where you lads heading?"

"Dallas," said Doc. He felt sympathy for the man. Cuthbertson had no idea what he and his laugh were up against

in Raider. He could only cross his fingers and pray that
Raider wouldn't attack the poor man. If only there were
some way to bring his laugh down an octave and smooth
it out.

On they rolled, the driver cracking his whip every so
often, keeping the pace at the ordained eight miles an hour,
wheeling up great clouds of fine alkali dust that merged into
one cloud, wrapping like a counterpane around the coach.
It seeped in through the sides of the drawn leather curtains,
invading the eyes, ears, nose, mouth, and clothing of the
imprisoned passengers.

Relief awaited them. Pulling into Montague, dust and
all, under suddenly blackening skies, a downpour struck.
It lasted less than five minutes, but managed to effectively
dispel the dust, wash down the horses and coach, and, when
it let up, enable the passengers to roll up the curtains and
admit some fresh air. At the first stop no one bothered to
disembark to stretch their legs, and within fifteen minutes
they were off again, their intermediate destination a way
station, where the team would be changed.

Two more way stations followed, and around one in the
afternoon they pulled into a home station. The passengers
piled out and into the dining room. Their haste was in vain;
the fare was atrocious—cold fried ham, three-quarters fat,
colder fried potatoes glistening with grease, ancient garden
peas, near-rancid butter, and homemade bread so stale it
threatened to shatter Raider's teeth. Sitting opposite Doc,
he was unable to resist commenting.

"This slop ain't fit for a hog," he observed.

His fellow passengers nodded and agreed with their eyes.
The station manager came over to him.

"Somethin' wrong?"

"You call this food?"

"It's all we got, pilgrim." The man patted his ample
stomach and smiled. "Keeps me goin'."

Raider handed him his plate. "Take yourself a little further."

"Aren't the ham and potatoes a trifle elderly?" queried
Cuthbertson. "Were they cooked this year?"

He laughed. The others stiffened. Raider started to say something and stopped. A bearded man in buckskin shirt and trousers had come in. He looked as if he had been riding hard, his boots and his person coated with dust. The manager went quickly to him. They talked in low tones. Raider caught one word only.

"Comanches!" he burst out.

Doc rolled his eyes ceilingward. "Rade..."

But the cat was out of the bag. The other passengers, three women among them, blanched as one. Perceiving their reaction, the manager returned to the table.

"Nothin' to get nervous about, folks."

"They're a little far east, ain't they?" asked Raider.

Doc glared. "Let the man speak, Rade."

"They've been seen here'bouts, but only jes' a huntin' party. Nary a sight o' war paint, bonnets, or such."

The shotgun spoke up. "We spot any, I'll be ready."

"Oh, hell yes," piped Raider. "Up on your perch there you can pick 'em off like jackrabbits."

"Rade..."

"Comanches, Doc. The bloodiest tribe alive! Worse'n Apaches. These folks should at least know what they're gettin' into." He faced the manager. "They should."

"They do now," said the man. "Wouldja like a refund on your ticket, Mr. Spleen?"

Cuthbertson laughed his laugh. Rather than stiffen the assembly, it appeared to relax them. Raider had risen from his seat. He sat back down very slowly.

"Comanches is still Comanches, Doc."

"Stop talking and eat."

"I didn't wanna upset nobody."

"Eat."

"I just think folks oughta know what they're gettin' into."

"Eat."

"I'm no damn scaremonger."

"Eat," said Cuthbertson.

They had covered almost half the distance to Dallas, with Hutchins situated just south of it, and the only feathers to present themselves to view were in the wings and tails of prairie chickens and an occasional quail. The sun was setting over the distant Davis Mountains, they had put Lewisville behind them, and Dallas beckoned when, rounding a turn, the driver pulled up sharply.

"Whoa, whoa!"

Raider leaned out the window. Standing on a ledge were three masked men, each showing two six-guns. A fourth man came scrambling down and approached, shotgun in hand.

"Visitors," said Raider. And smiled.

"What's so funny?" asked Doc.

"I haven't got a cent—no wallet, no watch, nothin' but a secondhand four-buck iron. It they're welcome to."

"You're overlooking something. What about your life?"

This last was a trigger. The interior of the coach exploded in a ferment of agitation. The women screamed, the men scrambled to hide their valuables. Cuthbertson jumped up, bumping his head, sitting back down hard.

"Everybody out!" bawled the masked man with the shotgun.

CHAPTER NINE

The passengers filed out, hands upraised, their reactions to the holdup varying from fear and trembling to frustration, even anger.

"This is disgusting!" boomed Cuthbertson irritably. "Illegal, unfair, uncalled for. You be careful with those firearms. If anyone's injured, even in the slightest, your eventual sentences when you're brought before the bar of justice, as most assuredly you will be, will be increased fivefold, tenfold!"

"Will you shut up!" barked Raider.

"Tell him, cowboy," said the shotgun. "Listen to the man, dude. You, messenger, what are you holding that thing up over your head for? That supposed to be a perch for birds?"

His companions guffawed. The messenger dropped his shotgun, which was quickly confiscated by one of the gang, the three having descended the rock.

"Let's hurry this up," said the shortest of the four to the leader.

"Shaddup. Okay, folks, do like you're told and nobody bleeds. Ladies first, everything on the ground right by my foot here. And don't let me see any shiny little derringers or peppermills. Guns make me nervous."

Again his companions laughed.

"Reg'lar merry-andrew-in-the-parlor, ain' he?" whispered Raider to Doc too loudly.

"Shhh."

"You say something, cowboy?" asked the leader, approaching Raider.

"Just mentioned you boys sure seem to know what you're about."

"We're about picking the lot of you cleaner than Sunday's pullet."

Another laugh. Ladies first, the passengers took turns adding their valuables to the pile. The strongbox was thrown down, blown open, and emptied.

"Mind you play square and give us your all," said the leader. "When you're done we're going to conduct us a little inspection. Anybody found holding out'll find himself in the soup for fair."

The warning prompted a sudden and spirited return to the pile by three of the first four passengers. The holdup was speedily completed, cleanly and professionally conducted every step of the way. Valuables and guns, including Raider's and Doc's, were added to the pile, the short man was sent to fetch the horses hidden behind the rock, and the loot was crammed into the leader's saddlebags. Mounting up, they galloped off.

Two of the passengers ripped their hats from their heads, hurled them to the ground, and stomped on them viciously. One of the ladies, fanning herself vigorously with her hanky, gave up the effort and fainted into the alert Cuthbertson's arms.

"I'm goin' after 'em, Doc."

"Oh no you're not."

"They got our guns, our money, your watch an' stickpin. We get to Hutchins we sure 'nough can't wire his nibs for money, not the way things been goin' lately."

As he spoke he walked away. He confronted the driver. "Let me have the loan o' one o' your nags."

"I can't do that, brother. 'Gainst company regulations."

"So's holdups. Give me one, I'll deliver it to the depot in Dallas before sunup. Honest Injun, cross my heart. An' get you your iron an' money back in the bargain."

"Well..."

"Good boy."

Doc continued to protest, but the disapproving stares of the other passengers, the driver, and the messenger soon discouraged him. Like it or not, Raider's mind was made up. Two minutes later, in spite of his aches and pains, their presence dulled by his anger, he mounted up and was gone.

"Everybody back in the stage," bawled the driver. "Next stop Dallas."

The holdup men had a good half-mile lead on him, Raider figured, but familiar with the habits of the breed as he was, he was fairly certain that along about now they would probably be slowing down, never dreaming they were being followed. They headed directly west into the blazing eye of the sun. He rode low, urging the stallion to greater speed, the wind whipping them both, the dun-colored, brush-littered land flying by. The setting of the sun did not seem to lessen the heat of the day. It occurred to him that he had not stopped sweating since Wichita. The town came sweeping back to mind: Broadway, the restaurant, the two holdup men, Gilmore gut-shot and dying on the floor.

What a West. It was getting so you couldn't even sit down to breakfast without trouble sitting down alongside. It was getting so half the population had taken to victimizing the other half. At the rate things were going it would soon be three-quarters against one-quarter. The trouble was, as he saw it, a holdup was so damned easy of execution. Surprise was on your side. It was quick, generally smooth, profitable, no overhead to speak of, no taxes, money. Sometimes even a small fortune in a few exciting minutes.

"Lazy man's way to wealth, sure 'nough."

Turning the coin over, he examined the other side, his and Doc's. All the danger, the excitement, the stress, surprise, and satisfaction, perhaps, but nothing like the profit. The agency paid them barely enough to survive on, and getting reimbursed for expenses, even those honestly incurred in line of duty, was like pulling the teeth out of a healthy grizzly. Allan Pinkerton had to be the tightest man outside of Scotland alive. To him money was blood, and parting with it was excruciatingly painful.

"Cheap son of a bitch!"

All the more reason to catch up with the four and pick them clean right back. Tit for tat. Far ahead he could see dust rising straight up a hundred feet, then bend off sharply in the face of a current of air. He veered off the road left, slowing slightly. All he needed was for one of them to look back and sight his dust. One empty holster against eight full ones and a twelve-gauge was not odds, it was calculated suicide.

He followed them for two hours, until darkness. Reading the Big Dipper circling the North Star, he put the time at ten o'clock when they finally pulled up. Hobbling their mounts, they built a fire and started supper. Then they got out the loot to examine it.

Raider hobbled the stallion a safe three hundred yards upwind of their fire. Down on all fours he crept forward to within about a hundred feet, taking cover behind a convenient thick growth of mesquite. He waited for what seemed like half the night, the sky clouding over, obliterating his clock, his stomach grumbling, the coals of his indignation glowing, threatening to burst into flame. He eased his ire with cursing. Meanwhile the outlaws examined their loot, ate their beans, drank their coffee, passed a bottle around, and turned in. Not even bothering to post a lookout.

"Nothing like confidence. Bastards!"

Presently all four arrived at their respective dreams, snoring lustily. Raider marveled at the sweetness of the sleep that a clear conscience ensured. He took a deep breath and crept forward.

Hutchins was Deadwood. A fraction of the population, perhaps, and, unlike Deadwood, not narrowly confined by the adjacent terrain to a single main thoroughfare, but just as dirty, noisy, and disgusting overall. Doc had retrieved their horses in Dallas. He had also picked up a copy of the *Dallas Morning News*. In it he found a follow-up story on Bass and Collins's most recent activities. Four days earlier the pair had stopped a Houston & Texas train and gotten away with a mail pouch filled with $40,000 in cash and

gold certificates. The item went on to say that the locals
were up in arms over the crime, and equally upset by the
law's inability to collar the miscreants. The mayor of Dallas
was quoted as advocating enlisting the aid of the Texas
Rangers. In their early days the Rangers had hunted cattle
rustlers and bank robbers, along with pursuing Indians and
Mexican troops, and had had a powerful hand in the shaping
of Texas. But after the Civil War the original Ranger force,
totaling about five hundred, had been disbanded, and it was
not until 1874 that they were reactivated by Governor Richard
Coke—mainly for the purpose of stamping out the gangs
of Mexican bandits who crossed the Rio Grande to rustle
the stock of the gringo ranchers. In Doc's view, suggesting
the Rangers be assigned to collar Bass and Collins was
impractical, although admittedly his opinion was to a degree
colored by the fact that he and Raider had failed to even
catch up with the two, let alone apprehend them.

And the only way he could see to change Mr. Storm
back to Mr. Bright would be to finish the job. Without
assistance, thank you.

He stabled the horses, registered at the Hutchins House
Hotel, and repaired to the nearest halfway-decent-looking
restaurant with the intention of dismissing forever the memory of his midday meal. He sat in a corner alone at a bare
table studying the grease-spotted menu under the impatient
eye of the waitress. Occasionally, he threw a glance at the
front window in hopes of spotting Raider.

"You want to order?"

"The veal looks good."

"Outta veal."

"Ham?"

"No ham."

"The chicken, then."

"Just sold the last one."

"I don't want steak. I'm just not in the mood."

"It's all we've got."

"Have you got another restaurant in town?"

"Nope."

"Let me think. I know, how about some steak?"

• • •

Raider stopped and flattened about twenty feet from the dying fire. To his left the leader lay snoring and snuffling under his blanket; beside him were his saddlebags crammed with the loot. Get his iron, thought Raider. Get every gun in camp, empty all except the newest of the lot, confiscate it—"trophy of the chase"—tie up the bastards, swipe a saddle, scatter their horses, and...

To his right the short man suddenly snorted and sat bolt upright, licking his lips and mumbling. Raider stiffened, flattening as low as he could get. The little man got to his feet, breathing huskily, resumed snoring, and extended both arms in front of him. He began walking slowly around the fire, narrowly missing a sleeper as he passed, then a second man, grazing the sole of his boot going by. Raider looked on in awe. The man reached the far side of the fire and was coming around. The leader lay squarely in his path. Raider began scrunching backwards. Around came the sleepwalker, step, step, step, snoring, licking his lips wetly. Straight up to the sleeping man he came. He bumped into him and fell headfirst over him, waking him. Up he scrambled, cursing, awakening the sleepwalker.

"What in hell do you think you're doing, Virgil? Sleep-walking again, ain'tcha!"

"Wasn't neither."

"How the hell you think you got over here, stupid ass-hole. I told you to quit it, didn't I? Christ Almighty, last time you walked straight into the damn cook fire, burnt your toe. When are you going to learn, for Chrissakes!"

"Hello, Tubal. What—"

"What! What! Get back over to your side and go back to sleep. I got a good mind to rope you down, stupid! Wake a man out of a sound sleep, scare the living daylights outta me. Jackass!"

He continued remonstrating with him. Virgil retreated. Raider lay with his right cheek buried in the sand, listening, taut as a bowstring, fearing that any second now Tubal would look around and see him.

"Tubal..."

"What now?"

Raider held his breath. Just shut up and go back to sleep, damn you! Of all the crazy things! If either one spotted him they'd surely blow his head off. Why not, out here in the middle of nowhere, no witnesses.

"Tubal, when we hook up with them fellows from up-territory are we gonna have to give 'em a share o' our goods, are we? I mean, they're ours; we-uns stole 'em. They don' desarve no share."

"Of course we don't divvy with them, stupid. Only what we get when we make our deal and start riding with them. From then on."

"That's good."

"Go to sleep, and for Chrissakes stay put!"

"Okay."

A long moment of silence followed, broken only by the steady thumping of Raider's heart in his aching chest and the dulcet murmur of the breeze. The stars twinkled over-head. So close did they appear Raider almost imagined he could hear them crackling.

"Tubal . . ."

"Shaddup, damn it!"

"Jus' one more question. When we do hook up with Bass an' the other feller, who'll be callin' the turns, you or them?"

"We won't make a move without my say-so. Now, if you open your mouth one more time I'll come over there and kick your head into little pieces!"

At the mention of Bass's name Raider drew in a breath sharply. Change in plans, sudden and drastic! There'd be no scattering their horses, no tying them up and leaving them for the sun to bake and the nearest lawman to ride out and collect. No sirree! Continuing to lie motionless, he listened intently. The night wore on. Virgil dropped off almost at once. Tubal took longer. He lay muttering to himself, stewing, belittling the lack of good help "in the business," the need to rely on "boneheads and misfits and idiots who can't even sleep lying down!"

Step by step Raider began reconstructing his strategy.

• • •

Doc dawdled over his coffee, continuing to study the street in hopes of sighting Raider. When he did not, his thoughts flew back to Deadwood and Lydia-Mae. Yes, he had loved her. Still did, perhaps even more than when she was alive. Raider had given his feelings for her short shrift, refusing to believe he could be serious. But he was. Never more. Apart from his feelings of love, he now felt a deep and abiding sympathy and a growing distress at the realization that in a very real sense she had died because of him. He had indirectly caused her death. The assignment and his necessary role in it, bringing Raider and him in contact with Bass and Collins, automatically placed her in the middle, for which she had paid with her life.

"Dear God!"

He felt sorry for himself as well, reflecting morosely that a man can spend half his lifetime searching for his ideal in a woman, spend his whole life and never find her. But he had found Lydia-Mae. Had known her for, what . . . ? less than two weeks, only to lose her.

Nobody but children and poets looked for fairness in this life. It had no more to do with anyone's existence than the stars have to do with the blossoming of a daisy or the death of a dog. No connection whatsoever. Life was entirely the luck of the draw; the longer he lived the more he was convinced of it. Some people enjoyed the sun over their heads from the day they were born to the day they died. Others never knew anything but rain. Most people's lives fell somewhere between the two, as did his own. Until this rain. He assured himself that it would rain from now on.

The door opened and two very old men came in. Old in every respect—in their carriage, the slowness of their movements, the manner in which they spoke, each one's slow reaction to the other's words, weary, time-worn, their days dwindling down to few, their lives lived. They took the table next to him, nodding, mumbling greeting.

"A good thing, too," said the taller, heavier one. "Make an example of them."

"I agree."

"A public hanging's just the ticket. Newspapers'll play it up. It might discourage others from lives of crime."

"Some of the young pups."

"Let's hope. I was here in '51. We never had anything like what you see now, people robbing and killing. Back then a man could leave his house and his door wide open. Oh, somebody might drop by while he was away, get themselves something to eat, drink from his well, but they wouldn't steal anything, wouldn't harm a stick. Today I don't know what the world is coming to, neighbor stealing from neighbor."

"'Tain't neighbors so much as outsiders. You're right, they got to be discouraged. Hang Bass and Collins in front of every man, woman, and child in the county. Like that double hanging, those two murderers up in Leadville, Colorado, last year. Ten thousand people watched that one. It was in all the papers. I'll wager it put the fear of God into a few rotten hearts."

Doc cleared his throat, drawing their attention. "Excuse me, gentlemen, I couldn't help overhearing you mention Bass and Collins. Sam Bass, right?"

"And Joel Collins. They finally nabbed 'em."

Doc's heart beat faster. "Are you sure?"

"Sure as can be. They're sitting in the calaboose in Mesquite this very minute. Trial's tomorrow."

"That courtroom'll be packed tighter than a bale o' cotton," observed his friend.

"How were they caught?"

"On the old Double-T spread, just outside Mesquite. It's been abandoned for six or seven years. They were hiding out."

"Posse surrounded the place, ordered them out, out they came meek as Moses. They found the Houston & Texas Railway mail pouch and every penny. Talk about red-handed."

"You heard this?"

"It's all over the county. Be in all the papers tomorrow."

Doc lurched to his feet, his chair scraping loudly. He

put money down, finished his coffee, thanked the two men, and practically ran out the door. He stopped the first passer-by, a boy about eleven in denims, bare feet, and a hat too big for his head.

"Sonny, which way is Mesquite?"

He jerked his thumb over his shoulder. "Cross the Trinity River up past Balch Springs. About ten miles. Five cents, please."

Doc gave him a dime and hurried off.

The chorus of snoring had become so loud Raider could barely distinguish the distant hooting of a great horned owl. Satisfied that all four were once again fast asleep, he stood up. The effort sent a shock wave of pain coursing through his body, gathering in his chest. The ride over from the stage was only now beginning to exact its penalty. He pushed his head back slowly, tentatively, cracking his neck, allaying the stiffness. Crouching, moving on his toes, he approached Tubal and silently slid one of his six-guns from its holster. He took the twelve-gauge and the saddlebags crammed with the loot, which were lying alongside him, and moved stealthily off to the nearest of the four horses. Its saddle lay on the ground close by. Hefting it up onto his shoulder, he started back toward the fire, toward his own horse hobbled far back in the darkness. He was passing Virgil when again he jerked up to a sitting position. Up came his arms as before. Up came Raider's hand, gripping the barrel of Tubal's Peacemaker. Down it came hard, hammering Virgil's temple. Back he fell groaning.

"Sweet dreams."

He walked on. He found his horse, freed it from its hobbles, saddled, and rode away to the east, pulling up about a quarter of a mile from the campsite. Two minutes later he set the clock of his brain for sunrise, closed his eyes, and slept.

The sun's appearance did not awaken him. A mocking-bird perched half-way up a nearby tree loudly went *tchock, tchock, tchock,* then burst into its beautiful song. Raider sat up aching so much that for a moment he thought he was bound in steel wrapping. He was starving. He should have grabbed what was left of their beans before getting out, he thought, but at the time he had too many other things on his mind. Rubbing the sleep from his eyes, he cast a wary glance in their direction. The land between rose slightly so that he couldn't see them, but their cook-fire smoke was visible, smudging the amethyst sky. He chuckled, wondering what Tubal's reaction had been upon awakening to find one of his guns missing, as well as the loot and the saddle. He'd probably blamed Virgil, who seemed to fill the role of whipping boy. Virgil's head had to be aching furiously. Maybe he'd accused Tubal of belting him; maybe they'd argued. Then again, perhaps Virgil didn't dare argue. Tubal was clearly the boss.

He moved forward, crouching, until their heads showed. He got down on his belly and watched. They had evidently been awake some time, he gathered; the shock at discovering their losses and any bitter discussion that would have followed seemed to be over with. They were finishing breakfast. Presently they saddled their horses—all but Virgil, who, to his annoyance, was assigned by Tubal to ride bareback. They mounted and rode off.

Raider followed.

CHAPTER TEN

The elderly diner's comparison of the courtroom in Mesquite to tightly baled cotton was apt, reflected Doc, squeezing his way forward through a knot of standees in the rear. His aggressiveness attracted dark, disapproving stares. He eventually gave up trying. A man about six foot four with shoulders like a barn door stood directly in front of him. The clerk barked for quiet and announced the judge. His Honor entered and rapped his gavel. The barn door effectively blocking his view, Doc could see none of this; he could only hear it. The judge called upon the prosecutor, who stood up and briefly outlined the case for the benefit of the jury.

"Your Honor, I would like to call the defendant, Samuel Bass, to the stand."

"Ac-cused to the stand!" bawled the clerk.

Doc leaned one way, then the other, accidentally pushing the man to his left harder than he intended. He glared at him and muttered, drawing the attention of the barn door, who turned. Just enough to permit Doc a brief glimpse of the witness chair and its occupant. The man sitting in it was about Raider's size,—young, hard-looking but clearly frightened. Doc gasped.

It was not Sam Bass.

"Your Honor!" he shouted.

The gavel rapped loudly; the crowd turned as one man.

"Your Honor!" repeated Doc.

"Who's that back there interrupting? Clement go back there and get that fellow. You there, yes you with the derby. What do you mean, yelling out?"

"Judge, that man in the chair is not Sam Bass!"

"I tolt ya! I tolt ya! Praise merciful God in heaven, at last somebody believes me! I ain't him! M'name's Alduous Roy Perrine, I sweah 'tis!"

No doubt persuaded by the expression of confident authority on Doc's face, the men in front made way for him. He emerged from the standees and hurried up the aisle. The crowd babbled loudly; the judge hammered for silence.

"Quiet down else I'll clear this courtroom!" Doc stood before him. "What in red hell are you talking about, stranger?"

"He's not Sam Bass. I've seen Bass. I've been closer to him than I am to you now. My partner and I have been tracking him for a week, all the way from Deadwood."

"He's loco, Tacitus!" snapped the clerk.

"Shut up. Who are you, mister?"

Doc started to respond, stopped, and lowered his voice. "Judge, can we step outside and discuss this privately?"

"We'll talk right here. And it better be good. I don't tolerate interruptions in my courtroom. Answer the question, what's your name?"

"Operative Weatherbee, Pinkerton National Detective Agency," rejoined Doc quietly.

"Pink . . . Let's see some identification."

"I . . . I don't have it. I was on the stage coming down from Ringgold. We were held up and cleaned out just outside Dallas. Wait, I do have something." Searching his pockets, he found the neatly folded telegram received from Wagner in Chicago. "This came from the agency. 'W W' stands for William Wagner, the office manager."

"Horsefeathers! You pulling my leg? This says plain as day you're a drummer with the Hercules Plow and Harvester Company."

"That's our cover," said Doc between clenched teeth, bridling his impatience. "See these letters?" He indicated NAZINOTY. "They stand for Hutchins, N for H, A for U.

Each of these is six letters further on in the alphabet from the corresponding letter in Hutchins."

"I'll be damned. Did I understand you to say you've got a partner? Where is he?"

"Tacitus..." began the clerk.

"Don't interrupt. Can't you see I'm busy?" He pounded his gavel. "Quiet in the court, or everybody goes! You, Bass, whoever you are, stop fidgetin'."

"Operative Raider. He's out chasing the bunch that held us up. He's a good man, Your Honor. He'll get them. Probably already has, and brought them into Hutchins."

The judge fish-eyed him. "Is this on the level?"

"On my oath, Your Honor. This man is not Bass. He doesn't look anything like him."

"What about his sidekick over there?"

Doc turned. The co-defendant, white-faced and even younger than the man on the stand, sat wide-eyed and sweating.

"I can't say. I've never seen Collins." He briefly detailed the shoot-out in the brothel–gambling casino, adding that, to his way of thinking, if Bass wasn't Bass, Collins wasn't Collins either. He brightened. "But these two could very well be in with them. No doubt are."

"What else would they be doing with the loot, right?" The judge plunged into thought, crinkling his brow like a walnut shell and scraping the side of his lower lip with his upper teeth. "You take a seat down there 'longside the prosecutor. Whoops, no more seats. Sit yourself down on the floor where I can see you." He summoned the prosecutor as Doc withdrew. "Proceed with the questioning. Let's get to the bottom of this thing pronto."

"I don't understand, Your Honor."

"I don't either. That chap says this one isn't Bass. Likely the other one isn't Collins. But it could be either one or both know where the real articles are, or where they're going. These two were found with the mail pouch, right?"

"Yes, sir. Exhibit number one, right there under the table."

"Okay, get on with it. Let's see if we can find out where

the real two are. What a mess. Jesus Christ, I should have stayed in bed!"

Once again he hammered for silence, then pointed his gavel at the prosecutor.

"Proceed."

"If you're not Bass, where is he?"

"I already tolt the marshal a hunnerd times. We both did. We don't have no idee where Mr. Bass or Mr. Collins has got to."

"You want this court to believe that they lit out and left you with that pouch full of Houston & Texas Railway money? Trusting souls, aren't they?"

"Mr. Bass tolt us straight out they'd be back to collect the pouch an' us'ns, me an' my brother, an' that we'd all three best be thar else two o' us'd wind up fulla lead."

The crowd tittered; the gavel rang; Doc shook his head resignedly, convinced that Bass and Collins had gotten away again. Word of this circus had to be spreading all over central Texas. They would have to be stone deaf not to hear about it. Losing the pouch would infuriate them, but better it than their freedom. In a way they could look upon the contents as the price of their freedom.

The trial, such as it was, was adjourned shortly and the two defendants ordered returned to their cells.

"Until the real Bass and Collins are apprehended. At which time you will be called upon to testify for the state against same."

The spectators were filing out when Doc approached the bench a second time. Standing up, the judge looked like a wrathful Rhadamanthus, peering down at him out from under his enormous brows, which in color and composition resembled miniature porcupines.

"Judge, with your permission I'd like to question those two in their cells."

"What for?"

"Sir, they looked pretty shaky out here on view. The one behind the table looked worried to death. Both looked intimidated. Questioning them in their cells, they might not feel quite so self-conscious. We've got nothing to lose. If they tell me anything, I'll be happy to tell the marshal. He can even sit in on the questioning if he wants."

"That's up to him. Okay, let's give it a whirl. Tell the marshal I gave you permission."

"Much obliged, Your Honor."

The two prisoners were lodged in the same cell. Both recognized Doc the instant the deputy brought him in, and their faces wreathed with suspicion. He had stopped on the way to invite the marshal to join them, but he had other business and declined.

"My name is Weatherbee," said Doc amiably, offering his hand to first one, then the other. "I may be able to help you. You." He nodded at the one built like Raider. "You're Alduous? And you . . . ?"

"Minot Sherman."

"Ain't nobody 'live can hep us now," moaned Alduous, wringing his hands and rolling his eyes in appeal to powers beyond the ceiling. "They's gonna string us up for sure. Catchin' us with the pouch an' all . . ."

"Nobody's going to hang you. It's possible you could even go scot-free."

"Possible!" exclaimed Minot Sherman.

"If you cooperate. I can't promise you, but it certainly won't hurt your case. You've got to trust me."

"Alduous already tolt that prosecutor feller we don' know where Mr. Bass an' Mr. Collins went."

Doc dug out an Old Virginia, offering the case to each of them in turn. Minot Sherman accepted one. Doc lit it for him, setting him choking.

"Let's backtrack a little. And please, try and relax, nobody's going to hurt you. You were in on the Houston & Texas Railway job." They nodded reluctantly. "Who selected the hideout?"

"We-uns, they din't know 'bout it nohow."

"Anybody else in on it?"

"Just us four," said Alduous.

"Anybody get hurt?"

"Nobody kilt. Mr. Bass hit the clerk over the head with his gun butt."

"You got away and rode back to the Double-T. Then what?"

"We counted the take an' ate an drank some," said Alduous. "Then, long 'bout midnight the two o' them buckled on their hardware, put on their hats, and says we're ridin' out. Minot Sherman ast where. Mr. Bass jus' snickered kinda—he has a way o' snickerin' 'steada answerin' when he don' wanna."

"And they left. Let's go further back. How'd you get mixed up with them in the first place?"

"Knowed Mr. Bass from Denton County back when," said Minot Sherman.

"You've ridden with him before. You don't have to answer that. I take it he approached you."

Alduous nodded. "Up to Gorza. We was jus' tads. Back then he, Mr. Bass, was like mah idol."

"Mmmm. So when he showed up this time you came down here with him. Okay, now think hard—it could very well save your skins. You and they must have talked a good deal from the time they found you until they rode away from the Double-T. You were together, living under the same roof. I want you to try and recall every place-name they mentioned, in whatever context. Cities, towns, hamlets, names of canyons, rivers, lakes, any rendezvous, anything. Just in Texas. To put it another way, was there ever any favorite place they frequented?"

"Big Spring," said Minot Sherman.

"Big Spring!" Doc's mind raced back to Montague and Sheriff Matt Gorsline. Big Spring, indeed. Was that where they'd gone? It did seem a long way to separate themselves from the $40,000. Why would they? Why not take it with them?"

"How far to Big Spring?"

"Far," said Alduous. "Clear 'cross the state, more'n three hunnerd mile."

Doc paused and put the pieces together. "They robbed the Union Pacific office there sometime ago. What else might they go back for?"

"Mrs. Collins."

He started. "That's it!" Half rising from his stool, he sat back down slowly. "It could be." He sighed wearily. "I don't know, it's all so iffy, it's trying to put myself inside their heads, practically think their every thought as they think them themselves. Did either one mention when they might come back to the Double-T?"

Both reflected on this, then slowly shook their heads.

"But they will," said Alduous. "They wouldn' leave the money."

"Not necessarily. They'd certainly weigh the risk against coming back. Then too, they could send word back to you to bring it to them. As far as that goes they could conceivably leave you two sitting on it for a year and a day. The money's the part I can't figure. Why wouldn't they take it with them? It's not cumbersome. It could easily fit into saddlebags."

"Mr. Bass trusts us," announced Minot Sherman proudly.

"So it seems. Can you remember any other places?"

They exchanged glances. Alduous shook his head.

"Okay, I guess that does it."

"Are they gonna let us go now?" Alduous asked.

"Not right away, I'm afraid. They still have to locate your friends. When they do, we'll see." Their faces fell. "Buck up. Cross your fingers. The thing you have to remember is that nobody in Texas wants you two. Bass and Collins are the prize plums."

He left. Thirty minutes later he was back in Hutchins. He went straight to the hotel. No, Mr. O'Toole had not yet arrived.

CHAPTER ELEVEN

Raider followed the four at a safe distance all day, carrying his aching ribs and the gnawing hunger under them with him. The sun was standing high overhead when he spotted a jackrabbit crossing his path within easy range. He was tempted to pot it, save it for supper, skin and fry it, but the shot would only attract their attention.

They bypassed Boyd, then Gibton. By sundown they were nearing Ketchi Creek. He calculated that they had traveled about eighty miles almost directly west from the site of the holdup. They crossed the creek, sloshing through the shallow water; he followed. About half a mile farther on they took a sharp right, headed north about four miles, then turned left off the road. Ascending a rise, they crossed it and headed down into a shallow valley covered with abundant grass that spread in every direction. This was the heart of north-central cattle country, he knew. On the opposite side of the valley, overlooking it, perched a rambling frame house. Smoke lifted from the chimney into the swiftly gathering darkness. Raider cut to his right, heeled the stallion, and, circling the rim of the valley, approached to within two hundred yards of the house. Dismounting, he hurried forward on foot. The four holdup men had already arrived and gone inside. Down on his belly he took in the lay of the surrounding land. Off the far corner of the house lay a crescent of boulders—good cover—and round about were scattered patches of dwarf and scrubby oak.

The front door opened and two men emerged. Raider
squinted and recognized Tubal and Sam Bass.

"At friggin' last!" he muttered, consciously reluctant to
swear, too appreciative to Lady Luck for her so long delayed
recognition and smile in his direction.

It was well over a hundred miles back to Hutchins for a
tired and hungry man on a tired horse. He didn't arrive until
well past midnight. Dismounting in front of the hotel, his
knees nearly gave way as he touched down. He had to lean
against the hitch rack for support and flex one leg and then
the other to restore circulation. Shouldering the loot-filled
saddlebags and bringing along the twelve-gauge, he went
into the hotel. The desk clerk sat with his head down on
the open room book, snoring contentedly. Raider eased the
book out from under his cheek, found Mr. Blaisdell's signature alongside 4C, and went upstairs.

Doc sat up, yawning, initially irritated at being awakened
out of a sound sleep.

"Get up. Get dressed."

"Forget it."

"Are you deaf? I said I found the bastards!"

"You're sure it's Bass and Collins?"

Raider scowled, patently wounded by Doc's doubt. Doc
explained the reason for it, telling him about Alduous and
Minot Sherman.

"I seen Bass with these two eyes. Close enough to shoot.
It was him all right, no mistakin' that build, that rooster
strut. We got to get back there pronto; they could be fixin'
to pull out."

"How many are there?"

"Six. Whatta ya lookin' so worried for? We can take 'em
easy as pie. Tubal, that's the one with the shotgun at the
holdup, the leader, him and his bunch are stump dumb,
honest. The runt, Virgil, oughta be set out to play with a
string o' spools, for Chrissakes."

"Intelligence doesn't count when the shooting starts."

"We can take 'em. Surprise 'em. I picked 'em clean all

by myself." He held up the twelve-gauge. "Even this two-cannon. Got all the goodies back. Your .38, stickpin, watch, money, the works."

"We'll turn it all over to the local law in the morning and get a receipt. Our horses came in. You'll have to return the stallion from the stage team."

"Oh for Chrissakes, what are ya spoutin' off 'bout details for? We got to wind this up! Everythin' else can wait!"

"Let's not go off half-cocked. The first thing we should do is round up some help."

"Are you kiddin'? We're in deep shit with A.P. for stretchin' it out this long, givin' Bass an' Collins time to pull off six or seven more jobs. The only way we can get straight is to collar them, an' by ourselves, you an' me. Tubal an' his boys'll be a bonus."

"I don't know, Rade."

"I do! Get dressed."

Doc laughed and waved him away. "Get dressed. Look at you—you're so exhausted you can hardly stand. Have you eaten?"

"Oh, hell yes, I stopped at a loblolly pine an' had me a steak an' fries."

"Why don't you go out to a saloon and see if you can get a sandwich. Then get a room and some sleep. Good night."

CHAPTER TWELVE

Raider capitulated. Grudgingly admitting that hungry as he was he hadn't enough energy left to go back out for something to eat, he lay down before he fell down and slept the sleep of the long dead. Doc came barging into his room at ten the next morning. He had been up since seven, had returned the stallion to the Wells Fargo depot in Dallas, along with the loot, and shopped for groceries.

"Wake up, get up!" he boomed. "We've got to get moving. I got us some beans and bread and coffee to take along with us. There's no telling how long we'll be out chasing."

Raider was sitting up, kneading his eyes with his fists, tearing the cobwebs from his mouth with his tongue, wincing and flinching as his various wounds awoke with him.

"Feels like I been pulled through a damn knothole. What's the grand rush, for Chrissakes, they're not goin' no place."

"How do you know? You don't. Come on, Rade, stir your stumps."

"All right, all right, you don't have to beat me over the head!"

Doc sat at the foot of the bed. "Do you think you can find their place again?"

"Easy."

He dressed, they went out for breakfast, packed the supplies in their saddlebags, purchased a couple of boxes of cartridges for Raider's newly acquired Peacemaker and Doc's recovered .38 Diamondback, and also bought a quantity of

00 buckshot for the twelve-gauge. It was a virtually brand-new American Arms, twenty-eight-inch, three-shot, nine-balls-to-the-cartridge blunderbuss guaranteed to take a man's head off at anything under fifty feet, and inflict mortal harm anywhere else on his body from far greater range.

It was after eleven when they finally set forth. They spared the horses riding back to the valley, arriving about eight-thirty. There would still be light for upwards of an hour, estimated Raider, measuring the sun against the horizon. Dismounting under the crest of the hill, they climbed up for a look. The corral adjacent to the house was empty; Raider's heart sank.

"I knew it! I knew it!" burst out Doc. "We should have been here hours ago!"

"Oh, for Chrissakes, shut up. They ain't gone. They're just out stealin'. They're hardworkin' boys, Doc, they don't sit around countin' their money, they keep busy. Let's go down an' have a look."

"What for?"

"See what's inside. So we can tell whether or not they're comin' back."

"You just said they were." A curious expression had seized Doc's face, a dark and troubled look.

"You feel okay?" asked Raider solicitously.

"Marvelous." He sighed heavily. "Remember what you said just before we left Deadwood, about this case being sick in the middle and rotten around the edges? That was well put, Rade, and the reason it's sick and rotten is because we have so little control. Up to now."

"Not no more. It's nearin' showdown time. We'll catch the bastards here with their drawers down."

"I wonder. Do you remember what I said when we were leaving Wichita, about losing heart for the chase? I thought it was temporary, an understandable reaction to what happened. But I still feel it, and even stronger. I wish to God in heaven it was over. I'm scared, Rade."

"You? Bullshit!"

"I am. I don't care anymore; there's no challenge in it, no satisfaction, so my heart just isn't involved. At this stage in every case before, I begin to feel fire in my belly. A . . . a force impelling me to get at it, do it, wind it up. I don't feel anything like that now. What I do feel is . . . bad. No eagerness, no self-confidence, no fire."

Raider laid a hand on his shoulder. "I understand."

"Do you? I've gone yellow on you, partner."

"Stop talkin' nonsense." He eyed him sympathetically. "You want to drop out?"

"I'd be apt to."

"You can. Climb on your horse, ride to the nearest town, send in your resignation. I won't stop you."

"Let's drop it. Sorry I brought it up. Let's go down and have a look."

They approached the house from the rear, Raider in the lead. He was mulling over Doc's words. Doc was right, he thought, his heart *wasn't* in it. Hadn't been since Deadwood. Would it ever be again? Probably not. He was just going through the motions for old time's sake. Out of something like respect for all their years together and all they'd been through. When it was over, away he'd go.

"Outta my life."

"You say something?"

"Nothin'."

The back door was locked, but the window over the sink was partially opened. They climbed through. Dirty dishes sat in the sink, and on the sideboard was half a loaf of bread. Cold beans sat in a pot on the stove. Raider knelt and pulled up the cold-cellar trapdoor.

"They're not down there, Rade."

"The loot could be."

But he found only potatoes, apples, and a jug of red wine. They began searching the house. There were saddle-bags, somebody's hat, a four-day-old copy of the *Dallas Morning News,* more dirty dishes on the table in the front room, and half a bottle of whiskey standing on the fireplace mantel. Raider helped himself to a swig.

"They're comin' back," he announced triumphantly.

"They've stolen a lot of money. I wonder where it's stashed."

"Buried in the backyard?"

"I doubt it. I've got a funny feeling it's right here under our noses. It could be up in the rafters."

"What's that?" Raider went to a corner. A piece of worn and filthy canvas had been thrown over an irregularly shaped object. He pulled it off. It was a brass, breech-loading monobloc gun with the date 1866 stamped on each trunnion. Under the barrel sat an open crate of shells. Four were missing.

"What on earth do they want with a cannon?" mused Doc aloud.

"This thing could blow a hole in a vault door big 'nough to stick your head through."

"Oh, my God . . . !"

Doc had straightened and was staring out the front window. Raider looked. A horde of riders was pouring down over the distant rim of the valley.

"There must be twenty of them!" exclaimed Doc.

Raider scoffed. "No more'n eighteen at most. Let's get outta here. Grab that box o' shells." Doc started for the kitchen and the back door, ignoring the order. "Doc! I'm bringing the cannon; you bring the ammo. Do it!"

Doc tried to lift the crate and could not. He cleared out the top layer of shells and managed to raise it from the floor. He staggered to the back door and started up the hill, puffing and fuming under the weight.

"This must weigh two hundred! I'll never make it. I'll break something. I'll get a hernia! My God!"

"Keep movin'!"

Raider scrambled up the hill after him, pulling the cannon by its trailspade. Since the house blocked their view, the approaching riders were unable to spot them until they showed themselves above the peak of the roof, two-thirds of the way up the hill. Immediately, the valley rang with gunfire. Lead slammed into the ground all around the Pinkertons. Raider roared.

"Move, goddamn it, you're blockin' the way!"

"You said six. Six! There's twenty or thirty! Why do I listen to you? Why!"

Raider ducked as two shots whistled over his Stetson. With about fifteen feet to go to the top and safety, Doc dropped the crate, its ponderous weight springing all four sides. He dove headlong for the top, while shells rattled and rolled back down the hill. Raider let go of the trailspade. The gun began rolling back down. Cursing vilely, he scrambled back, caught hold of the handspike, and started back up. Lying prone just over the top, Doc peered down at him. Bullets continued to whine about them. A shot rang off the cannon; another found the heel of Raider's left boot, knocking it cleanly off.

He stiffened momentarily. "Goddamn it! See what you made me do?"

"I didn't do a thing!"

"Come back down here and get this ammo!"

"Pick some up going by."

"Bastard!"

With a last burst of strength triggered by his sudden anger, Raider pulled the piece up to the top and, one hand still clutching the trailspade, threw himself down beside Doc.

"Of all the yellow-bellied bastards!"

"Didn't I admit it?"

"Shut up and give me a hand with this thing."

They pulled it over, out of sight of the attackers. The shooting stopped abruptly.

"Now, go back down and get the ammo," snapped Raider. "Quick, while they're reloadin'."

"What reloading? They've stopped because they can't see anything to shoot at."

"All right, all right, I'll get it."

"You stay where you are."

Doc removed his derby, set it on the ground in front of him, and pushed it slowly up to the top. A rifle cracked; the bullet plowed cleanly through the crown. He fingered the hole.

"What the devil did I do that for?"

He inched back down. Raider held up the shotgun.

"There's three shots in here. Take it, get back up, and start blastin' when I tell you. I'm goin' down after two or three shells quick like a snake."

"It's suicide, Rade. They're sitting there cocked and ready, waiting for one of us to show."

"Perchin' up here two against twenty's suicide."

"Not if we get out of here."

"Do like I tell ya, goddamn it!"

"If anybody's going back over it'll be me!"

"Here!" Raider slammed the twelve-gauge against him. Doc slammed it back. "Cover me, plowboy, while I cover myself with glory."

Before Raider could say another word Doc had scrambled back up to the top. Raider pulled himself up alongside.

"Here goes nothing!" barked Doc. Over he went.

The watching outlaws let fly. Raider answered, loosing three thunderous blasts. Doc snatched up two shells, reached for a third, pulled back his hand from a slug that landed right where his palm had been, and, turning, lunged for the top, tossing the shells ahead of him. Raider pulled him over and down amidst a fierce volley.

"Good boy. For Chrissakes, you only got two!"

"I'm sorry, I'm sorry," said Doc acidly. "I swear, there's no pleasing some people!"

Raider loaded the fieldpiece, tilted the barrel down as low as it would go, pushed the piece back up to the top, and, aiming it straight at the back door, scrunched down.

"Hang onto the trail with both hands. She'll jump a good six inches. Keep her steady."

Doc grabbed the trail and pressed down with all his strength.

"Here she goes!"

Raider jerked the lanyard. The gun boomed, the ground shook, smoke billowed about them, the shell slammed cleanly through the back door. The center of the rear roof rose, and the back of the house blew outward.

"Good Lord," gasped Doc, rising slowly to survey the damage. The survivors were pouring out the front door, mounting, riding away. Raider emptied his Peacemaker, hurrying them along. He grinned and patted the muzzle of the fieldpiece.

"Damn! Damn thing's hotter'n hell. Sure does pack some wallop, though."

"Eleven, twelve... Amazing. One shell and at least seven or eight are dead."

"Or wounded. Reload the shotgun and let's have a look."

The outlaws had crowded into the kitchen and the rear bedroom adjacent to it. Six of them had taken the full force of the blast. All were dead, bloodied, battered, and broken. Two had their heads blown off, one his left arm. The stink of cordite hung in the air; blood ran down the walls. Raider recognized only one of the deceased: Virgil. He lay on the cold-cellar trapdoor, his left side shattered from shoulder to hip, a gory mass of meat and bone shards. The sight of him sent a wave of nausea through Raider's stomach. Doc turned from the grisly sight.

"Get the horses, Rade, I want to take one last look around for the money."

"Screw the money. We catch up with them we'll get it quick enough. Let's get after 'em."

Bass, Collins, and the others had nearly a ten-minute head start. Having taken off in all directions, they drew together and were now riding bunched, as evidenced by the single fat dust pillar rising behind them. They were heading west toward Salt Creek, but an hour into twilight their dust turned sharply south. By nightfall they had crossed over into hilly Palo Pinto County.

"Where do you suppose they're heading?" asked Doc, pulling up alongside Raider.

"How should I know? Only thing I do know is they're not just joyridin', they got someplace in mind."

"What's the next town?"

"What does it matter, they'll sure as hell bypass it. Unless they got a job lined up."

"What's the town?"

"The county seat, Palo Pinto. It's dead center the county, 'bout twelve or thirteen miles ahead. They been goin' a good pace a pretty long time, I got a hunch they'll be stoppin' anytime now. It's plenty dark, no moon. 'Nother fifteen minutes we won't be able to see outside our eyes."

"Good. When they stop, one of us'll ride on into Palo Pinto, get ten or twelve good guns, come back, surround them, and take them."

"Got it all figgered out, ain'tcha?"

"Can you think of a better strategy?"

"A dee-mented jackass could. I say we let 'em stop, eat, and bed down; we do the same. Come sunup we get up afore they do, take their lookout, an' get the drop on the lot before they're half awake. Run 'em into Palo Pinto, jug 'em, an' wire old A.P. an' Wagner that we're all wound up."

"Rade . . ."

"Doc, why ring in outsiders? We come this far by ourselves, on our own, why can't we finish the job? If you're gonna quit, don't you wanna go out with a feather in your cap?"

"How do you know it won't be a bullet in my head?"

"Bullet'll get you a feather for sure. Hey, look!"

The outlaws had pulled off the road up into a mass of boulders and outcroppings, affording near-perfect concealment. They hurriedly dismounted and ran their mounts into crevices and behind the larger boulders out of sight.

"Bastards are gettin' set to bushwhack us." Raider heeled his grulla sharply left. "C'mon, let's get round behind 'em."

They pulled up ten minutes later, their horses heavily lathered and blowing hard. Raider dismounted.

"What now?" asked Doc, eyeing his partner jaundicedly.

"Let's eat."

"You. I'm going into Palo Pinto and get help."

"Bullshit."

"Don't try to stop me, Rade."

"Your horse is bushed."

"I'll spare him. See you. And while I'm gone, don't do anything stupid."

Wheeling about, Doc rode off into the blackness, sped on his way by a salvo of swearing that was generously laced with allusions to the color of his liver. He smiled grimly to himself. Was Rade right? Had he, at this late date, actually turned yellow? Perhaps. Perhaps losing one's heart for the fray automatically invested one with a yellow streak. One thing he knew with certainty: His visit to Deadwood had changed him, had turned his brain around inside his head. Now everything he looked at—the world, the job, his relationship with Raider—he saw through different eyes.

It was she who had changed him. For the first time in memory he was aware of a whole new set of values, all based on their worth, their meaning and importance to *husband and wife*. And a continuing career with the Pinkertons was out of the question in this new scheme of things. Worse than useless, it was detrimental, entirely alien to the life their shared future promised. Now there would be no "shared future," but having acknowledged the existence of such an alternative, one that excluded outlaws, guns, danger, pain, and bloodshed, the benefits *just getting out* offered looked increasingly attractive.

There was another aspect. Looking into the future, ten, fifteen years hence, if he stayed on he would be doing the same job, running the same risks, courting the same disasters, earning the same pay, only older, wearier, slowing down, and disgusted with it all. But he would be trapped in it, unable to extricate himself. He was educated, intelligent, still relatively young; the career possibilities were endless. To work, that is to say to be on call 144 hours a week, week in, week out for the meager pay of a Pinkerton operative, to work like the proverbial dog, hurrying to catch up with the bullet waiting for him with his name on it, was nothing less than insanity. People worked from eight to five, weekends off, vacations, time to relax, to spend with their loved ones, to enjoy. This job was twenty-four hours around the clock. Raider loved it; for all his bitching and whining it was his dish of tea.

But not his. It may have been at one time, but no longer. Not since Deadwood and Lydia-Mae Breed. This newly structured, drastically different perspective on life was her legacy to him. For her sake, for the sake of what might have been for them, for himself, in his best interests he would resign. Turn his back and walk away from it. Go back east, start fresh. Now, before it was too late. Nothing Raider could say would dissuade him. The man was his best friend, probably the best he would ever have, the brother he had never had. They would always be Damon and Pythias, sharing fond remembrance of the wild past, but be that as it may, their lives were not inextricably linked. They could part company. He could walk away. He would.

Palo Pinto beckoned, a scattering of lights piercing the gloom. The sheriff's office was locked. His pounding on the door awoke no one. A grizzled-looking, shabbily dressed man wearing a broad-brimmed, disreputable-looking hat that flapped like a crow's wings with every step crossed the street and came up to him.

"If you're looking for Sheriff Owensby he's over to Slocum's." He pointed back across the street at a saloon, its presence announced by a sign badly in need of painting: SALOON. No name, Slocum or otherwise. Doc thanked him and walked off.

Slocum's Saloon looked as if it needed a good hosing down. The sawdust on the floor was black, the mirror behind the bar hadn't been wiped in ages, the place reeked to gagging of body odor commingling with the vague but distinguishable smell of vomit. The bartender pointed to the rear.

"That's him with the handlebars playing stud. There with his back to the wall."

Doc approached the game and politely waited for the hand to end.

"Sheriff Owensby? May I have a word with you?"

"Who are you?"

Doc walked around the table and displayed his I.D. card. He explained. Owensby anted for draw, got his cards, and half listened. He was not in the least interested, Doc decided, conveniently dismissing the gravity of the situation.

"We need ten or twelve good men."

"Any o' you boys wanta volunteer for a posse?"

His question was ignored. A fat, red-faced man sitting opposite him cleared his throat and his nose.

"I can open."

"'Fraid you're outta luck, friend."

"Sheriff, my partner's out there alone. These men are wanted all over central Texas. There are half a dozen prices on their heads."

"They ain't done nothin' in Palo Pinto County."

"They will if they're not apprehended. They're here now, ten or twelve miles from here."

"I'm in. Friend, when they do something, I'll get after them. It's my duty to, I'll see to it. Until they do . . ."

The rapidly thinning last strand of Doc's patience snapped. "We can stop them before they do anything!"

"I just asked for volunteers. You heard. Two cards, Sylvester, and make 'em decent for a change. I'm losin' my shirt. I just asked, you saw, nobody's interested. We're busy."

"Sheriff . . ."

He got his cards. "Damn it to hell! That's the third bobtail flush I pulled tonight! I'm out. Mister, I can't help you."

"It's your job!"

The discussion was beginning to attract attention. Owensby glared. "Are you gonna leave off pesterin' me or what? You're gettin' me techier than a teased snake. If you know what's good for you you'll get the hell outta here. Goddamn, look at that, a full boat! You're luckier than a pig in shit, Woody! What in hell you been doin', goin' to church?"

Doc was not about to give it up. There was too much at stake. He cast about for an empty chair; there was none. He moved to the other side of the sheriff. The dealer called for seven-card stud.

Raider watched Doc's dust settle, reiterated his opinion that he was "one yellow son of a bitch" for the tenth time, then set about hobbling the grulla. Checking his Peacemaker and the shotgun, he set out for the rocks.

"Bastard. You pick a great time to go down in your boots on me. Leave your partner high, dry, and outgunned. Leave it to a woman to ruin a man. Startin' with Adam an' Eve in that garden. Yellow's your color, Weatherbee. I always knew it was, just took a little longer time than I figgered to show through your hide."

He ventured to within a hundred feet of the rocks, crouching, staying low, straining his eyes, looking for the man on guard. There'd be at least one, maybe two or three. They knew they were being followed. It wasn't the best time to go for them, while they were still wide awake and alert. Better to wait till just before sunup. But to hell with that.

"All the years together don't count for snap beans to you, do they, 'partner'? Sweep 'em all behind the spittoon. Goodbye, good luck, to hell with you, see you round. That's a true friend, all right. When I think of all the times I saved your yellow skin. So many times I can't count that high. This is the thanks I get. Yellow as baby shit, that's what he is, what he sure 'nough turned out."

He froze. Not forty feet from him sat a man with his rifle across his lap, his knees drawn up, head down on his forearms.

"Yellow doesn't come to a man outta the blue. No sir, it's deep down inside him. All it does is come to the surface, like sweat. His heart, his guts, his liver get so crammed with it they got to let it out. Out it comes, collectin' along his backbone. Shows up like a vein o' pure gold. With his shirt off you can spot it a mile away."

He came up behind the man, walloped him back of the right ear with the butt of the shotgun, and caught him as he groaned softly and fell over. Seizing the rifle, he set the stock on the ground at an angle and stomped it in two, all the while continuing to unburden himself of his feelings.

"He's just usin' her an' what happened as a excuse. Son of a bitch never did have any heart for the business. Heart meanin' guts. Always did hold back. Always lookin' for the least dangerous way. Like right now, ridin' into Palo Pinto. A dollar to a nickel says the sheriff'll turn him down cold."

Hauling out the man's six-gun, he emptied it and threw it as far as he could. Then he went looking for other guards.

"Sheriff's got no stake in this, why stick his nose in? You're wastin' your time, Weatherbee. If you know what's good for you you'll get your yellow ass back here an' finish the job. Shit, as if he ever knew what was good for him."

Circling the rocks, he found only the one guard. One down and how many to go? Doc had counted twelve riding away. Eleven now, and he'd be out cold for a good half hour, maybe longer. Maybe he'd busted his skull.

"My biggest mistake was lettin' you come along. I shoulda left you up to Deadwood. This'd be all wrapped up an' tied with a ribbon by now if I had. All you do is get in the way an' delay things. Startin' with that dumb train ride down from Scotts Bluff. Goddamn dumb waste o' time."

He found three men sleeping around the dying fire. He approached them stealthily. He didn't recognize any of them.

"Good riddance, I say. Maybe I'll get me a real partner, somebody with a little fire in his gut. Somebody'll pack a real gun 'stead of a toy popgun. Somebody dressed like a human bein' 'stead of a store window dummy. Somebody who can ride a horse without bitchin' 'bout his cheeks an' his crotch like a old woman. Somebody with balls. A man."

One after another he hammered the three sleepers foreheads, relieved them of their weapons, destroyed their rifles, and cached their pistols in crevices where they would be impossible to retrieve. Four down, eight to go.

"Damn agency owes me that much, a decent partner, somebody I can bank on. Never could on you, Weatherbee. The one thing I could count on with you was not bein' able to count on you. Like droppin' that crate. Perfect example. When the goin' gets hot, Weatherbee gets out, drops the crate. What the hell good is a gun without shells? I bust my balls draggin' the damn thing all the way up an' over an' he drops the crate. Asshole!"

Climbing a rock, he lost his footing and skittered down the face, landing hard, the shotgun clattering to rest beside him. The noise woke two men close by.

"What the hell was that?"

"Somebody's up here."

They were suddenly looming over him side by side, like twin angels of death. He gulped and sprang, throwing himself at their legs and toppling both. Winding up on his back, he drew and fired—just in time, catching the bigger one full in the gut, his gun dropping from his hand. Again he fired, catching the other one in the throat.

"Sons o' bitches! Damned spoilsports!"

The others were well awake. He could hear voices and clambering about all around him as they went for their weapons. He looked around. Ten feet from him an enormous rock, the largest of the grouping, beckoned. he ran for it, jumped over one of the bodies, swinging around behind it.

"Yellow can save a man's hide but kills his pride. It's a known fact. He'll never be able to look himself in the eye in a mirror again. I sure would hate to live with the weight he's got to live with on my conscience. I can look me in the eye; always will. Yellow-bellied an' backed like a goldfinch. Disgustin'! Sickenin'! Son of a bitch!"

He found a ravine just wide enough to back into. He sat down in it, pulling his head down between his shoulders, the shotgun cocked and ready to welcome the first intruder. He strained his ears. They were still moving about looking for him. Finding their unconscious and dead buddies all over the place.

"Old A.P.'ll hand his head to him, curly-brimmed derby, hole an' all. One thing the old man can't stomach is a man who loses his balls, throws 'em away, a turncoat, a traitor. Benedict Arthur, that's him, that's you, Weatherbee!"

A man rose directly in front of him.

"Evenin'," said Raider politely and blew him away.

Another came up behind him. Spotting him as he aimed, Raider fired. The hurried shot ripped through the front of his hat brim, stopping him just long enough for Raider to get in a second shot. He emptied the chamber into his chest, blowing him heels over head.

"Let's see, how many is that? Two an' three..." He cradled the empty gun and counted on his fingers. "Five an' two is what... seven? An' two more. Nine." He stopped.

He could hear hooves pounding. Up he jumped. He could
see nothing, but riders were leaving. Down out of the rocks
he ran.

They were heading south, Bass, Collins, and Tubal. It
had to be. He had recognized none of them among those
he had knocked out or shot. He ran as fast as he could for
his horse, cursing every step of the way.

"This is your fault, Weatherbee, pure an' simple. A yellow partner an' a man's bound to wind up doin' everythin'
himself. Tryin'. Bastard! Son of a bitch!"

CHAPTER THIRTEEN

Doc came away from Palo Pinto empty-handed, Owensby's vitriol ringing in his ears. He had threatened to clap him in jail if he didn't leave him alone.

"Stupid coward, a disgrace to his badge. Yellow!"

He headed back to Raider at a lope, thoroughly disgusted with the situation. It wasn't bad enough they were saddled with a seemingly impossible task, outnumbered and out-gunned; on top of that, they couldn't even get the local law to cooperate. Allan Pinkerton would hit the ceiling when he heard. And he'd make sure he would. He'd come down on Owensby like a brick wall. He'd cite him in print as a disgrace to his office. For all the good that did them at the moment.

The sound of hooves and the sight of dust jolted him out of his thoughts. Instinct prompted him to pull off the road. Vaulting over the rain ditch, he pulled up about twenty yards from the road, turning his horse in time to catch sight of three riders hurtling by. He recognized Bass. He couldn't see his face, but there was no mistaking his build. Only three? Perhaps the others were coming up behind. He waited, frozen in his saddle. A long moment passed; he changed his mind. He took off after them.

His horse was tired, having enjoyed less than fifteen minutes' rest while he and Owensby had argued. Bass and the others cut off the road on the approach to town, then for some unknown reason changed their minds and got back onto it. Into town they barreled. Their indecision gave Doc the chance he needed to catch up. They stopped in the middle of town and ran their horses down an alley.

He passed the same alley, hitched his horse, and followed them cautiously on foot, making his way down between the buildings to the backyard of a three-story frame building with a long, zigzagging stairway attached to it. The outlaws were nowhere to be seen. There hadn't been enough time for them to climb to the top floor, he reasoned, which left him the choice of one flight up or the ground floor.

Their horses stood panting and steaming, glistening with sweat, one wall-eyeing him and pounding the ground with its forehoof. Gathering their reins, he led all three down the row of buildings to a barn and got them inside. Then he went back to the building and stood a moment, considering the situation. He rejected the idea of barging in after them. Bass would recognize him on sight; they'd be three, possibly more against one. He envisioned himself coming out feet first, his hat on his chest.

He went back up the alley to the street. The little town was brightly and clamorously alive. Up the street and across it stood Slocum's Saloon. Owensby was probably still losing and grousing, shirking his duty. Doc found himself almost wishing that Bass and Collins would dip their greedy fingers into Palo Pinto if for no other reason but to stir the sheriff to action. They'd be doing him a favor. The way his cards were running, another hour and he'd be flat broke.

He stood at the corner of the building pondering his next move. A buckboard rattled by. He glanced overhead just in time to catch sight of Bass standing at the window of a front room on the second floor. He no sooner recognized him then his shadow spilled down the window as he backed out of sight.

Doc glanced down the street after the retreating buckboard, then up the street. A lone rider was coming, dusting along at a good clip. He ran out to him.

"Rade!"

He caught his reins and the grulla stumbled to a stop, snorting, flinging her head.

"Will you look what the cat dragged in," growled Raider icily. "Mr. Butter Britches himself in the flesh. I woulda thought by now you'd be on a train headin' for Chicago, sittin' composin' your letter o' resignation."

"We still have a case to wind up."

"If you'll kindly let go o' my headstall I'll get to windin' . . ."

"Nonsense. You haven't the slightest idea where they are."

"You do?"

"Right up there in that front room." He indicated. "Now, would you mind getting back out of their line of sight?"

He practically dragged man and horse to the head of the alley.

"Sometimes you surprise me, Weatherbee."

"Oh, shut up. I don't need another of your patented lectures on integrity and loyalty to the agency. Will you ever get it through that thick skull of yours that neither of us owes Allan Pinkerton or his agency a thimbleful of loyalty? It's a job, Rade, that's all it is. We haven't taken the veil. We work, we're paid, we can quit anytime we please. Did you know that the average career span of a Pinkerton operative is only—"

"No need to apol'gize."

"I'm not!"

"Sounds like it. If your conscience is botherin' you, you can't blame me."

"It's always bothered me; that is, it has up to now. It bothers me to waste the best, the most productive years of my life running around like a crazy man after other crazies."

"Don't feel bad. Turnin' yellow's not the worst thing in the world. There's rape, there's baby stealin' . . ."

Doc pulled him down bodily from his horse. He landed hard on his rear. Doc jerked him to his feet and delivered a solid shot to the jaw, slamming him against the building.

"Son of a bitch!" yelped Raider.

"One more word—one—and I'll beat you to death."

"Okay, okay." There followed a long, heavy silence, the air between their eyes charged with electricity. Raider was the first to relax. He rubbed his jaw and flexed it gingerly.

"I owe you, Weatherbee. Enough bullshit. What now? How 'bout we scamper up there after 'em?"

"No!"

"Shhhh, Chrissakes."

"Why walk into the lion's mouth?"

"Why not? They sure as hell ain't expectin' us."

Raider moved around the corner to the front of the building, backing away into the street in order to see the window.

"You stay here an' kick it aroun' another hour or so. I'm goin' on up."

He started down the alley. Doc caught up with him.

"Rade . . ."

"If you're comin' come, only leave off bendin' my ear. You talk an' talk, it goes in my ear, drips down into my stomach like tobacco juice, an' after a while I get so pukey sick I wanta heave. So kindly jus' shut the hell up!"

They ascended to the second-floor landing. The back door was unbolted. Inside narrow doors confronted them on both sides of the hallway.

"This here's a cathouse," observed Raider. "Hear the gigglin', the springs squeakin'?" He sniffed. "Smell the u-de-cologne?"

"Oh."

A single door loomed at the end of the hallway just beyond the front landing. Doc nodded. Approaching the door, they took their positions on either side of it. Raider readied and raised the shotgun.

"Oh, for God's sakes, must you?" whispered Doc. "It could be unlocked, you know."

"If it ain't, it will be."

Doc's hands made it only halfway up to his ears before Raider fired. Pain pierced their eardrums; it was like a bomb detonated inside a barrel. Smoke rose. Raider kicked open the door. Two women in their underthings stood cowering and screaming. Doors flew open up the hall behind the two

Pinkertons. Worried, painted faces under mountains of gold and platinum, jet and purple hair appeared.

The outlaws were not in the room.

"I knew it!" exclaimed Raider. "I knew one o' us shoulda stayed by the front door. I tol' you!"

"You told me nothing. If we'd stayed put like I wanted they'd have run right into our arms!"

"Bullshit!"

"When are you going to learn not to go off half-cocked?"

"Don't go blamin' me. It was you kept me down in that goddamn alley talkin' my ear off my head, lettin' 'em—"

A loud muffled explosion stopped him. Doc brushed past the two whores, staring out the window.

"The bank!"

"Down the front way!" snapped Raider. "Move!"

They elbowed their way unceremoniously between two patrons coming up the stairs, Raider very nearly sending the shorter of the two flying over the railing. At the foot of the stairs stood a tough-looking man in formal attire, his light blue eyes as hard as nailheads, staring icily at them out from under heavy lids. He appeared tense, his hands curled into fists and ready to swing.

"What the hell's goin' on!" he bellowed.

"Just leavin'," explained Raider.

"Hold everything!"

Raider swung the shotgun forward, aiming it straight at his chest. "Get outta the way or I'll blow you out."

The man glowered fiercely and stepped aside.

"Excuse me," said Doc as he passed.

Their attention diverted by the bouncer, neither noticed the four cowhands coming up the front steps. They bowled straight into them, knocking three flat. Raider landed on his game shoulder and bawled in pain, while the twelve-gauge landed on the sidewalk.

"What in blue hell!" sputtered one of the upended cowhands.

Doc helped him to his feet. "Sorry, sorry."

"Why'ncha watch where you're goin', for Chrissakes!"

"Why don't you!" rasped Raider.

"Never mind, Rade, come on."

The brief delays proved costly. By the time they got across the street there was no sign of Bass, Collins, and Tubal. The lock on the front door was broken, the safe blown, the back door wide open. Raider ran to it muttering. The night wind greeted him, ruffling his hat brim. He strained his ears and thought he heard the faint sound of hoofbeats. He couldn't be sure. Stripping his hat from his head, he dashed it to the ground, cursing vilely.

CHAPTER FOURTEEN

To Raider and Doc's consternation they discovered that both
their horses and someone else's, a roan gelding beside which
Doc had earlier hitched, had been stolen by the outlaws.
Bass, Collins, and Tubal's own mounts were still in the
barn where Doc had hidden them.

They mounted and rode out, electing, at Doc's insistence,
to head northeast for Parker County, thence across the south-
east corner of Wise County and on into Denton County.

"It's possible that's where they're heading, Rade."

"It's possible you're fulla shit."

"Think about it. We know Denton County is Bass's old
stamping ground. He suddenly finds himself short of man-
power, thanks to your heroics. What better place to recruit
than amongst his old friends?"

"How do you know he wants to recruit? How do you
know he isn't all wound up and headin' for the border?"

"All he has on him is what they just stole from the bank."

"Why would he run away? Why leave all the other loot
behind? It could be back at that ranch in the valley. We
never did get to look for it thoroughlike. They could be
headed back there."

Doc shrugged. Within seconds, almost as if fate herself
were eavesdropping on their speculating, a fork in the road
presented itself. The way left wound sharply around a grove
of trees, heading what appeared to be straight for the valley
and the hideout. They pulled up.

135

"What do you think?" asked Doc.

"Whatta you asking me that for? You're doin' all the thinkin', as usual. How in hell am I supposed to know which way they're headin'?"

"Don't get mad. If we take the right, what's the next town?"

"I don't know."

"Come now, you know Texas like the palm of your hand."

"Mineral Wells."

"And how far to Denton County?"

"A good sixty miles, and that's to just over the line."

Doc pondered, hammering his fist lightly against the pommel of his saddle. "I've got it. We'll split up. You go to the hideout and look around. I'll head for Denton. When you're done at the hideout, when you've found the loot or they've shown up, whatever, you get out and head straight for Denton. I mean the town. We'll meet at noon tomorrow in the local watering hole. If you don't show I'll take it to mean you're still occupied at the hideout, okay? At which point I'll ride over and join you."

"You make it sound like a hop, skip, an' a jump. You're talkin' Texas miles, you know. Besides, chances could be good. Be great they're neither place. They could be halfway to Waco. They could be headin' for New Mexico, Oklahoma..."

"Ever the optimist. Goodbye!"

Doc heeled his horse and barreled away down the right-hand fork. Raider pulled left and took off at a canter. The air was damp and unusually still, filled with an expectancy of sorts. Any moment now, he imagined, the blackness overhead would part and rain would come spilling down in buckets. But it didn't. On and on he rode, coming at last onto the road he had followed before from the rocks into Palo Pinto. Presently the scrub-festooned land began rising gradually. He climbed to the top, pulling up and looking down upon the shattered silhouette of the house. The wind came up, whipping his hat and the horse's mane, a big and big-barreled, flea-bitten gray, the sort of mount a man walks right by at an auction, but serviceable, willing to run, and no more than four years old.

He started down into the valley, through the grass grown golden in the heat of summer. Dismounting, he entered the house. The corpses lay where they had originally fallen, the nauseating stink of death filled his nostrils. He gagged slightly and fought off the sick feeling. The wall between the kitchen and the rear bedroom had been all but completely shattered by the blast. He found a kerosene lamp and lit it. He found Virgil, still lying across the cold-cellar trapdoor. The blood caking his shattered side had congealed and darkened in color. Raider went through his pockets. He found four paper dollars in an ancient wallet. In it also was a faded photograph of a plain-faced, slender, and shapeless young woman, his wife or sweetheart. Her hair was braided and wrapped around the top of her head. She displayed a worried expression, prompting Raider to imagine that the picture had been taken just after an argument between the two over Virgil's choice of career. She had had good reason to worry, though no longer. Had been right to worry, for all the good it did her. He put the four dollars in his own wallet and put Virgil's back in his pocket. He was about to straighten up when he remembered Virgil's shirt pocket. He reached inside it and found a piece of paper folded twice. Holding up the lantern, he studied it. It was a crudely drawn map of north-central Texas, embracing six counties west and south of Denton. Denton County alone was identified by name, but there were a number of tiny crosses within its boundaries and to the left and below it, like stars swarming about the moon. Roughly half the crosses were circled.

"Jobs pulled off, jobs planned, you betcha."

Curiously, none of the four crosses in Denton County showed circles around them, suggesting that Bass and Collins were saving them until last? Possibly.

He searched the other bodies, avoiding the two decapitated by the explosion, unable to stomach the sight of them up close. Each of the corpses carried a map identical to the one he had found on Virgil. Which wasn't all that bright, he thought. If any one of them were to be captured and

searched it would give away the whole operation. Still, it
could hardly be classified as a long-term project. Eight days,
ten at most would be time enough to hit every spot.

Poking through the kitchen, he found a few twelve-gauge
shells lying loose in a drawer. But no trace of the loot. He
went over the front room, concentrating on the chimney,
pushing an old broom up into it. It was empty of everything
but soot, which rattled down in quantity. He searched the
blown back bedroom. The side wall was severely damaged,
but not nearly as badly as the one separating the room and
the kitchen. The explosion had loosened floorboards in one
corner, he noted, but upon investigating the area underneath,
he decided that this wasn't so. The boards had been pulled
up. He found a number of paper straps of the sort used to
wrap currency, and a single twenty-dollar gold piece, over-
looked by the outlaws in their haste.

"They musta emptied this hole out soon as they got here,
while they were shootin' at us."

Where had the loot gotten to? If they had taken it with
them wouldn't it have been in Bass's and Collins's saddlebags? He himself was riding Bass's gray. They certainly
wouldn't have left here without their money.

Or had they recovered it earlier? If that were the case,
why should they come back? His weariness was muddling
his thinking; he gave up trying to figure it out.

Bringing the lantern with him, he went back outside. He
searched Bass's saddlebags. He found food and two nearly
full boxes of .45 cartridges, but no money. Not a dollar.
He dropped the shotgun shells he had found in the kitchen
in with the .45 shells.

Hoofbeats! He blew out the lantern and, slapping the
gray's rump with his hat, sent it galloping around behind
the house. Then he ran back inside, crouching, twelve-gauge
in hand at the front window.

Three men were approaching. His heart came alive, thud-
ding against the wall of his chest. It was much too dark to
distinguish their faces, but he had no doubt who they were.
Who they had to be. He let them come to within fifty yards,

smashed the window, shoved out the shotgun, fired, and ran to the still open door.

"Pull up, drop your guns, get your hands high, or I'll kill you!"

Before he even finished they had flung themselves from their saddles, bellied down, and begun returning fire. A slug lodged in the door as he moved to close it. A second shot kicked dirt in front of the sill. He slammed the door.

"Stupid bastards! Stupid me, I shoulda shot to kill!"

Glass shattered and rattled lightly to the floor. Head down, he duck-waddled back to the window, raised up warily, got off two more shots, and, lowering, moved to reload. And stopped.

"Son of a bitch!"

He was out of ammunition. Too late he remembered that he placed the loose twelve-gauge shells in Bass's saddlebag. He drew his Peacemaker and emptied it. Chancing a look out into the blackness, he couldn't even make out a silhouette. He continued shooting blind, emptying his gun a second time and a third, reloading from his belt, cursing in frustration as he did so.

Steps. Heavy. Behind him. Caught with his gun empty, he whirled.

"Drop it!"

He did so, rising slowly, lifting his hands.

A lone man came into the room. He was old, his hair and beard going from white to yellow, his face deeply seamed. A sheriff's badge glistened at his breast pocket. He held his Colt pointed straight at him.

"Drop your belt." He lit a match with his thumbnail, holding it up to examine Raider. "Get that lantern outside on the ground. Go on."

Raider did so. Handing him a second match, the sheriff ordered him to light the lantern. He did so and set it on the table.

"Who are you, Buster?"

"Name's Raider. Pinkerton National Detective Agency. Who in hell are you?"

"Sheriff Matthew Gorsline, Montague County."

"Good ways outta your bailiwick, ain'tcha?"

"Let's see some identification."

Raider handed over his wallet. Gorsline studied his I.D. card, but if it made any impression on him he failed to show it. He also failed to return the wallet.

"You got a partner?" he asked, his deepset eyes narrowing suspiciously.

"Weatherbee."

"That's the name. We've met. Where is he?"

"We split up. He's on his way to Denton County."

"What are you doing here?"

"Looking for the money."

"Oh?"

"For Chrissakes!" he snapped in exasperation. "You've seen my I.D. You know my partner."

"The question is do you? Is he your partner? It's possible you've killed them both, and walking around now passing yourself off as this—"

"—Raider. You're fulla shit."

"That too is possible. But how do I know for sure you're who you say you are?"

"Who do you think I am? Bass? Joel Collins?"

Gorsline wasn't listening. He found the map taken from Virgil. "Oh my, what do we have here?"

His two deputies came in waving similar maps. "Look what we found, Matt."

Gorsline compared maps. He shook his head gloomily.

"I got mine off the little guy, the one lying on the cold-cellar trapdoor," said Raider.

"This fella claims he's a Pinkerton, like that Weatherbee fella I told you about. He's got identification, but who can say for sure?"

"I say, goddamn it!" Raider broke in. "How's about we cut the horseshit and finish searchin' this dump? The loot's here."

"Who says?"

"It is. Look over here." He showed them the place in the corner of the bedroom. He told them about the fieldpiece, the shoot-out, their tracking the gang to outside Palo Pinto, the bank robbery. The sheriff continued to study him with a mistrustful expression.

"I'm tellin' ya the bald truth!"

"If you are, you got nothin' to worry about."

"What in hell's that supposed to mean?"

"It means I'm taking you back with us. I'm afraid I'm going to have to hold you."

"Bullshit."

"I swear, you do have a way with words."

"Just give me back my gun and I'll get outta your hair."

"Oh, no you don't. I may be overly suspicious, and you may think I am, but we've been running up against brick walls all over the map. This place and you are the first and only clues we got to where they're going, what they're up to."

"I'm no damn clue. You talk horseshit, you know that?"

"You've seen them, you claim you have. Put yourself in my place. I can't be too careful. You could have bush-whacked the real Raider and lifted his wallet. We'll search this place top to bottom, all right, but then you're coming back with us. You can squawk till you're blue in the face, but that's the way of it."

In the unplanned exchange of horses Doc had gotten a dark chestnut, strong as a moose, but only three-quarters broken. It liked to run, but in a direction of its own choosing. He overworked its bridle keeping it on the road to Mineral Wells.

The sun was coming up over Hickory Creek and the line of rugged, low-lying hills beyond it when he came upon a battered sign announcing Denton seven miles ahead. He splashed across the creek, climbed the hill, and started down the opposite side. Denton rose into view, crowned by a vivid pink sky.

He resolved to get something hot to eat, catch an hour's sleep, no more, and start combing the area. He sighed wearily. Duty of another sort also called. The Western Union office in the center of town had not yet opened for business when he rode by it, but after he had eaten and caught his catnap it undoubtedly would be. His conscience, already up and prepared for the day, urged him to get a wire off to Wagner in Chicago. Get it off before he and Raider linked up again. Allan Pinkerton must be seriously considering firing them by now. He had to at least let him know they were still alive, although in his present mood he would surely take that as bad news. Maybe he could cook up some not-too-farfetched nonsense that would lower his hackles.

It was ten to eight by the time he got out of bed, shaved, and prepared for the day's hunting. He went straight to the Western Union office.

TWO NEW ACCOUNTS AS GOOD AS LANDED STOP ONLY A QUES-
TION OF TIME STOP RECENT ACTIVITIES OF BOTH REFLECT UN-
USUALLY GOOD PROFIT FIGURES STOP AS SUGGESTED THEY
WOULD BE WELCOME ADDITIONS TO OUR LINE STOP EXPECT
CONFIRMATION BEFORE THE WEEK IS OUT

MB

He sent the telegram collect, left the office, paused out-side, and lit up his first cheroot of the day. The last one in his case. He examined the case for a long, poignant moment. It was all he had left of Lydia-Mae, all he would ever have, apart from the permanent ache in his heart and the already dimming memories of their brief time together.

He would give ten years off his life to hold her in his arms again and kiss her.

Yes, he would most certainly go back to Deadwood when this business was finished. And from Deadwood head east. Not get off the train until Boston.

Two men sat on a bench in front of the Western Union office, one with a crutch beside him, the other sporting a Gloucesterman's wraparound rope beard, a singularly un-common sight this far west of the Atlantic. He was busy whittling. A shapely, strikingly handsome woman sailed by, her plum-colored, frilly-hemmed skirts rustling around her unseen ankles. She was young but very much in command of herself, as evidenced by her posture and the no-nonsense look about her. The merest suggestion of rouge brightened her soft, white cheeks, and her lipstick put Doc in mind of Adelaide Parasol in Ringgold, although there was no physical resemblance whatsoever between the two. Both idlers touched their hat brims in greeting. Her eyes and Doc's met, and he too put a finger to his brim in chivalrous salute. She nodded, half smiled, and glided away, leaving the delicate scent of jasmine in her wake. He followed her with his eyes.

"You know who that was?" the whittler asked the crutch, his tone conspiratorial. "Emma Collins, that's who. Just got to town last night. I seed her gettin' off the train."

Doc caught the last name and tumbled it about in his mind.

"Come lookin' for her man," said the other.

"Must be," said the whittler.

"Excuse me, gentlemen," said Doc, abruptly conscious of a glow taking occupancy of and rising in his stomach.

They eyed him stonily.

"I couldn't help overhearing." They continued to stare. Neither spoke or appeared to want to. He had committed the unpardonable offense of eavesdropping. The punishment: silent rebuke and dismissal.

"Have a nice day," he said mildly, suppressing a chuckle.

He started after the lady. She had stopped to look in the window of a millinery shop. He stopped, stood puffing on his Old Virginia, then crossed the street. She resumed walking. He kept pace with her on the other side. She went into the Bluebonnet House Hotel. He stood across from it, finished his smoke, stamped the butt underfoot, straightened his tie, recrossed the street, and entered the hotel.

The lobby was deserted. It smelled faintly but deliciously of jasmine. The lady was nowhere to be seen. The clerk sat behind the front desk absorbed in a copy of the *Police Gazette,* his eyes protruding from their sockets, the tip of his tongue running over his upper lip. Whether he was reading something salaciously stimulating or viewing a scantily clad beauty, Doc could not tell upon approaching. Seeing him, the man slapped the paper closed and stuffed it under the desk, coloring slightly as he did so.

"Morning, sir."

"Good morning. Would you mind checking to see if there's any mail for Abernathy? Houston W. Abernathy?"

The clerk's face crinkled in puzzlement. "Are you a guest?"

"That's right. Checked in late last night. Houston W. Abernathy. Take a look, would you?"

"Yes, sir. Room number?"

"Four-D."

He turned to investigate 4-D's box. Reading the guest register upside down, Doc spotted Mrs. Collins's signature. Unfortunately, she had signed "Mrs. E. Collins." For Emma? Edward? Edgar? Impossible. She had to be Joel Collins's wife.

The clerk spun around. "Not a thing, Mr. Abernathy. But there's a delivery at nine-thirty."

"I'll be back."

"If anything comes in I'll send it up to your room."

"You needn't bother. Oh, by the way, wasn't that Joel Collins's wife I saw going upstairs just now?"

"That's right, sir. Fine figure of a woman, isn't she?"

"I should say."

"You a friend of hers?"

"Yes, indeed. We go way back, Emma and I. Say, if you don't mind, I'd kind of like to surprise her sometime later. We haven't seen one another since Kansas City a hundred years ago. I'd appreciate it if you didn't let on you've seen me."

"Ahhh."

Doc stifled a sigh and blocked out an unpleasant thought concerning the avarice of man. He produced a half dollar and pushed it across the desk.

"I haven't seen a thing, sir." The clerk grinned, retrieved his *Police Gazette,* and prepared to resume reading. "Too busy."

• • •

In the midst of misfortune compounded by equal portions of frustration and irritation Raider came to savor a mild triumph of sorts. He succeeded in talking Sheriff Matt Gorsline into returning his wallet. It would have been funny if it hadn't been so infuriatingly annoying. If the son of a bitch really did suspect it wasn't his, that *he wasn't him*, why in hell give it back?

He would go to his grave wondering how some people's minds worked.

"Not how, if."

Sheriff Gorsline riding ahead and the two deputies in line behind him did not hear. To their left a carpet of bluebonnets gradually merging with white wildflowers stretched away, butting up against the dominant tall golden grass. Ahead the land rose, and to the right a low hill broke the horizon. From its center rose a fat column of smoke, dirtying the bright blue sky. Gorsline picked up the pace. The narrow, deeply rutted road curved around the hill. Halfway into the curve a grisly sight jolted them—a farm wagon was engulfed in flames, hissing and crackling, and twenty or more Indians were milling about. Too late, Gorsline pulled up and started to swing about.

The savages spotted them, sent up a chorus of blood-curdling screams, and came barreling toward them. No hunting party these boys, reflected Raider, swallowing the stone of fear. The leader wore a spectacular warbonnet boasting fifty or more eagle feathers, each one decorated with bright stripes of beadwork at the base and tipped with a plume fashioned from the hair of a white horse. His braids were wrapped in beaver fur, and a porcupine quill bib hung from his throat. Like his warriors, he was stripped to the waist, and his chest, arms, and face were emblazoned with war paint. All their faces were broadly striped in black, the color of death. They carried lances, and Raider counted five rifles, ancient Springfields and Henrys, he guessed—ancient but still workable.

Their victims lay on the ground near the blazing wagon. A brave knelt beside one of the corpses and was taking the scalp, slicing to the bone, lifting the hair, holding it up triumphantly. Gorsline swore savagely and shot and killed him screaming.

"Jesus Christ," muttered Raider. "Didja have to? They're already comin' after us."

"Shut up and ride."

"Gimme back my gun."

Back down the road they hurtled, side by side.

"I can't do that," responded Gorsline, his tone apologetic.

"Goddamn it, man, you want me to die empty-handed? Is that what you want? Gimme my shotgun!"

He gave him back his Peacemaker. "You'll get your belt and cartridges when we light somewhere."

"If we ever get a chance to. These boys mean business. Why in hell did you have to spoil their party?"

Arrows flew by. A gun cracked behind them. The deputy bringing up the rear cried out, slumped in his saddle, and fell off, his ankle catching in his stirrup, his horse dragging him in the dust. Raider turned and emptied his gun. Gorsline one-handed the twelve-gauge, getting off two shots, the second dropping the brave at the head of the pack.

"They're gettin' closer," rasped Raider worriedly.

"Up ahead!" yelled the second deputy in the lead.

A mass of boulders beckoned. They deserted the road, reached the cover, threw themselves down, and dove behind the rocks. Arrows rattled around them like hail drumming. Raider sneaked a peek out from behind his boulder. The savages had pulled up about a hundred feet away. They appeared momentarily confused. The chief waved his arms and screamed orders. Collecting, they began circling the rocks at a gallop. Raider, Gorsline, and the deputy repositioned themselves as their attackers came around. Raider dropped two and the sheriff a third. The deputy shot and missed and shot and missed.

"Son of a bitch couldn't hit the ground through a four-inch pipe," groused Raider.

"What are they?" asked the deputy.

Raider scowled. "Indians."

"Comanches?"

"Likely. Strayed off the reservation and lookin' for blood. Sheriff . . ."

"What?"

"Toss me over the shotgun."

"You don't need it. You're doing nobly."

The Indians had given up circling. Assembling, they wheeled about, spread wide, and charged. Arrows rattled off the rocks, and a slug grazed the boulder behind which Raider crouched. On they came, galloping through the rocks, screaming their lungs out. Bunching his body, Raider fired straight upward, catching a brave in the nose, ripping it from his face, loosing a freshet of blood. The impact bowled him over out of his saddle; he fell, smashing his skull against the hardpan. Gorsline, too, killed one barreling by. The survivors, some twelve or fourteen, assembled on the other side, swung about, and came thundering back.

Raider's eyes were drawn to the deputy. He had taken a lance full in the chest and lay splayed on the ground, his face twisted in agony, his dead eyes bulging from their sockets. Gorsline saw and swore.

Once more the savages came galloping through. The chief's pony's forehoof came down in a rut and twisted. The pony's back gave way, and man, warbonnet, and all flew to the ground. Gorsline put a bullet squarely between the chief's surprised eyes, chortling gleefully.

But the loss of their chief goaded the warriors to new fury. Raider and Gorsline braced for a third charge, welcoming it, relishing the savages' vulnerability in the split second of their passing. But this time the Indians altered their strategy. Assembling in a fat cloud of dust well out of range, they dismounted and spread out in a straggling line to a distance of a hundred yards, flattening themselves in the foot-high grass and holding their fire.

"Watch the bastards," barked Raider. "Here they come."

"Shoot any moving grass," advised Gorsline.

"No shit!"

"You're pretty fair with a gun."

"I'm the berries with a twelve-gauge. Try me."

"You're doing fine. How many left, do you think?"

"Too many. Ten at least."

"How—"

A rifle spoke. A tiny red circle appeared dead center Gorsline's forehead. Up rolled his eyes, out came his tongue, over he rolled.

"Ohhhhhh boy."

He pulled himself over on his elbows to where the sheriff lay. Seizing the shotgun, he tossed it back to his rock and glanced about, looking for the horses. The one closest was his gray. He whistled to it. It turned its head, bobbed it, but did not move a hoof.

"Get over here, you flea-bitten hay bag!"

Again he whistled. The horse started for him. A barrage of arrows came flying past Raider as he pulled down. They struck the horse, dropping it to its knees and over on its side.

"Red bastards."

The gray lay about twelve feet from him. A rock half the size of a flour barrel offered the only protection between him, the injured animal, and the saddlebags containing the two boxes of .45 cartridges and the dozen or so remaining shotgun shells. Reloading his six-gun, he emptied it in a wide swath of gently moving grass. Up on his knees, crouching, he sprang forward, two, three, four steps, throwing himself down behind the prostrate creature's belly, a flight of arrows, a single lance, and two shots whistling over his head. He got out the ammunition and reloaded with one cheek flat against the ground. Then started back.

But the one thing he needed most he left behind. Luck. He was almost back to his rock when an arrow hit him in the shoulder, plowing squarely into the flesh knitting around his old wound. He groaned aloud; it was like a branding iron pushed deep. Landing on his knees, he rolled over. Clenching his teeth, he gripped the shaft and pulled. The head came with it, followed by spurting blood. Ignoring it, he threw another barrage at the sea of grass directly before him. Two lucky shots hit two unlucky braves.

To his surprise he found the shotgun fully loaded. And promptly emptied it into the grass.

Blood poured from his wound. It hurt so much that for a moment he was afraid he would pass out. Ripping off the tail of his shirt, he wrapped it around his shoulder, tightening it with his teeth, hastily knotting it. Then went back to shooting.

It had developed into a Mexican standoff. Every time he saw movement he fired. More often than not he hit his target. He killed two more, leaving . . . he couldn't be certain. But enough. At least five or six. Then he spotted two at the extreme ends of the twisting line. They were moving off at right angles with the obvious intention of getting around behind him. Concentrating on one, then the other, he blew them away with his six-gun. His success served to discourage the others. Suddenly the waving grass betrayed their retreat. He watched and waited for a full five minutes. All at once they sprang up from the grass about a hundred yards from him, ran pell-mell for their ponies, mounted up, and galloped away. Leaving their dead, Gorsline, Deputy One and Deputy Two.

Who, poor bastard, couldn't hit the ground through a four-inch pipe.

CHAPTER FIFTEEN

Doc very early decided and with the utmost conviction that Mr. Collins would come to Mrs. Collins, and not vice versa. He stood across the street from the hotel waiting for her to come out, intending, having nothing better to do with his time, to follow her about town. She might send a wire; she might meet someone, a go-between.

But she did not appear. As he stood idly waiting, a worried feeling established itself in his mind. He and Raider had worked together for so long, each had developed an instinct for the other's welfare whenever circumstances separated them. Akin to the sixth sense Dumas's Corsican brothers developed for each other.

Raider was in trouble, whether at the hands of Bass and Collins or others he could not ascertain, but in trouble he was. Standing, watching the hotel, the feeling took root and grew. In trouble, in need of help. He sighed. He hated to leave her. They could very easily return and find her gone.

Raider made it to the Chico road before collapsing in his saddle and tumbling to the ground. He lay in the rain ditch weak as water, his mind fuzzy around the edges, his eyes propped open by sheer willpower, deliberately staring at the sun. Oblivious of his plight, his horse stood greedily eating grass, swishing its tail contentedly.

"You're a son of a bitch, you know that? If you'da come when I called you this never woulda happened."

The horse nodded, but only to rid itself of a bothersome fly, not in agreement. Indifferent to his presence, it went back to its nibbling. He examined his wound. The bleeding had stopped, congealing in a badge-sized mass. He had lost a gallon of blood, he mused, most of it when he'd pulled out the arrow. The fire within still burned brutally. The sight of his wound sickened him slightly. He looked back at the sun; it swam before his eyes, darkened, and out he went, falling over on his good side.

He had no idea how long he was out, but when he awoke it was getting dark out, the sky where the sun had been as purple as sage, the breeze gentle against his cheek. A small boy stood staring down at him. He wore a straw hat and bibs two sizes too large for him. His feet were bare and filthy. He stood gaping, his little fists bunched behind his shoulder straps, a spear of grass protruding from the corner of his mouth.

"'Lo."

"Mmmmm."

"You hurtin'?"

"Bleedin' to death."

"Oh, pshaw!"

"Pshaw your ass."

Not in time he caught himself. Musn't foulmouth a child, he reflected.

"What's your name?"

"Aaron Howard Preston Gilhooly."

"Lotta name for such a little sprat."

"Ain't little." His mouth tightened, his small jaw jutting forth indignantly. "What's your name?"

"Billy the Kid. How 'bout gettin' me some water?"

The boy pointed. "Stream's over yonder. Ain't got no cup or nothin'."

"There's a canteen hangin' off my pommel there."

"You really Billy the Kid?"

"In the flesh."

"You can't be, you're too old."

"Mind your mouth."

"You hurtin' bad?"

"No, I'm just lyin' here catchin' my beauty nap. Canteen..."

He came back shortly. Raider grit his teeth and forced his eyes open. He drank sparingly, spilling most of it down his chin. He held out his hand. The boy poured his palm full and he slapped his face with it. It felt good, cool. Again he drank, then poured what was left on his wound.

"More?"

"Please."

By the time he returned Raider felt sufficiently invigorated to sit up. Texas swam about his head. He battled to remain upright, won, and shook away the dizziness. He managed an appreciative smile.

"Billy the Kid," said the kid.

"Like I said, in the flesh."

"You're a horse-faced liar."

"Tsk, tsk, tsk, such language. You live round here?"

He pointed toward the right of the road, toward Chico. Raider drank more water, sipping slowly, wary lest he heave it back up and with it what little strength it had restored.

"You dyin'?" asked the boy, worry bunching his freckled features.

"Jesus, I hope not."

"Can you see angels?"

"No."

"You're not dyin'." He seemed disappointed.

A lone rider was coming. He squinted up the road. It swam briefly under the darkening sky, steadied and defined the approaching man.

"Son of a... gun."

Recognizing him, Doc's hand went to his derby to hold it on, and seconds later he came thundering up, his horse rearing and pawing the air. He jumped down.

"Rade!"

Raider started to respond, was unable to, grinned feebly, and passed out.

• • •

Raider woke, his eyelids parting. He was abruptly conscious of pain. He closed his eyes, opened them a second time, his hands sneaking to his ribs. He was lying in bed fully clothed but for his shirt. His wound had been bandaged, but it was not the source of his discomfort. His lower ribs ached furiously on both sides.

"My ribs are busted."

Doc sat beside the bed smiling. "Just sore. I had to tie you over your saddle to get you back here."

"Man, am I hungry! How long I been out?"

"Six days."

"Oh, bullshit!"

Doc nodded at the night table on the other side of the bed. A napkin covered a tray. Raider sniffed.

"Steak!"

"Probably ice cold by now. Would you like me to feed you?"

"Just cut it up. I'll feed myself, thank you."

"It's already cut. Dig in."

Raider ate. Every mouthful seemed to add to his strength. The steak *was* cold, but the coffee was still hot in its pot. They filled each other in on what each had encountered in the hours preceding.

". . . Mrs. Joel Collins, Rade. That boy back in jail in Hutchins, Alduous Perrine, first mentioned her. She's come from Big Spring to join up with Collins."

"She still here?"

"Upstairs in Room 3E."

"Jesus, what a break!"

"That remains to be seen. Who knows if they'll try to get together?"

"Why would she come all this way? We gotta stick to her like glue."

The color was returning to Raider's cheeks, the dull, glazed look deserting his eyes. He threw his legs over the side.

"What do you think you're doing?"

"We got work to do."

"Stay put."

"What'd you do with my shirt?"

Ignoring his partner's protests, favoring his wound, he managed to get back into his shirt.

"C'mon, let's go see if she's still here."

"I'll go. Finish your coffee. Take it easy."

Doc went downstairs to the lobby. The *Police Gazette* devotee was still on duty. He scowled.

"Hello again," said Doc.

"You lied to me, brother, trying to make me think you were registered. Where do you get off, pulling my leg?"

"Sorry, just playing a little joke. No harm done, no hard feelings, okay?"

"If you're looking for her, you're out of luck. She's checked out."

Doc stiffened. He started to say something, changed his mind, and ran to the door. He looked up and down the street. There was no sign of Mrs. Collins.

"When? Where's she going?"

"Didn't say. Just checked out."

"Damn!"

He ran out a second time. Holding his derby in place, he raced toward the railroad station. A train was just pulling out. Up to the ticket window he ran.

"Where's that train heading?"

"Pilot Point. You just missed it," averred the man behind the bars.

Doc destroyed him with a glare capable of shriveling marble. So vicious was it, so intimidating, the man backed away a step.

"Won't be another along till ten past eight in the morning," he mumbled. "Good night."

Down came his shutter. Doc heard the snap catch inside and the pin being slipped through the loop to hold it. He turned from the window.

"Damn and double-damn."

Raider was waiting for him in the lobby. He listened to his explanation, shaking his head slowly.

"Nice goin', Weatherbee. You do good work. I'm proud o' you."

"Shut up. If you hadn't gotten in front of that Comanche arrow, if I hadn't wasted all this time hauling you back from the dead, feeding you, waiting on you hand and foot, this never would have happened."

"Oh, then I apologize!"

"Can you sit a horse?"

"Can a gnat bite?"

Ten minutes later they were on their way to Pilot Point, Doc muttering, decrying his miserable luck, fuming and seething, chafing and ranting. While his partner, discreetly keeping a good two lengths between them, laughed and laughed and laughed.

Raider stopped laughing in Pilot Point. It was past midnight and the train station was deserted. There was no possible way of telling whether the lady had gotten off there or stayed on for Tioga, Collinsville, Whitesboro or any one of a dozen stops east or west of the last named.

The half-hour ride north had taken its toll on Raider's depleted strength. Doc noticed, but refrained from comment. Instead he sighed heavily.

"Our bird has flown. Any suggestions?"

"How 'bout some shut-eye?"

"Capital, Rade, capital."

Their only link with the outlaws now broken, for want of a better place to go, they returned to Denton. Fate had dealt them, in Raider's words, a bobtail straight. It was a discouraging turn, but it was not the end of the game. They were still in Bass's home county. It was there, Doc was certain, they would eventually catch up with them.

They sat in their hotel room the next morning. Raider stared at the crude map he had found in Virgil's pocket until his eyes ached. It offered a choice of no fewer than twenty-six possible victim locales. Not one was designated by name,

156 J. D. HARDIN

but their locations and the distances between them gave him
a good idea of what they stood for.

Two more days crept by. At precisely ten o'clock in the
morning word exploded, careening from one end of Denton
to the other. The "new" Bass and Collins gang had held up
the Cattleman's Bank in Pilot Point, less than an hour's ride
from Denton.

CHAPTER SIXTEEN

Doc stood at the mirror combing his hair and otherwise sprucing up in preparation for leaving. Raider sat on the bed watching him, his expression thoughtful, as if something was bothering him greatly. Virgil's map lay before him.

"Get a move on, Rade, we've got to get back up there."

"No."

So stubborn sounding was the tone in the single word, it prompted Doc to turn and look at him questioningly. Raider shook his head.

"We're goin' about this thing all wrong. Stupid."

"We're going about it the only way we can."

"That's not so. We've been chasin', chasin', chasin' the three o' them all round Robin Hood's barn. *What we should be doin' is chasin' the loot.*"

"They're one and the same."

"They're not. Listen to me. Don't interrupt till I'm done."

"We're wasting valuable time."

"We're wastin' shit. So they hit the bank up to Pilot Point. The local law's after them, runnin' all over the place. They won't catch 'em; haven't yet. The three o' them an' whoever else they got to ride with 'em has likely gone to ground. They'll lay low for a few days."

"Then?"

"I'm comin' to it. Just relax an' listen, we're not goin' anywheres. Think back. First I'll tell you this. *I know where the loot is*. Think back to that night in the rocks where they stopped. Bass, Collins, an' Tubal got out before I could get to 'em. My horse was too far away, I couldn't get right after 'em."

"You could have taken one of their horses."

"I didn't. I wanted my little girl. That's not important. I was late gettin' after them, but you, comin' back from Palo Pinto, picked up their trail, right? Now you said you followed them an', at least at first, they started to skirt the town. Then changed their minds an' rode on in. Went straight to that cathouse."

"You think the loot is there?"

"It's got to be."

"I don't see as how it's 'got to be' anything of the sort."

"It's impossible for it not to be there. When they stopped and ran their horses down that alley out to the back they had to know I'd be right on their tail. They didn't know you were. You went out back an' . . . what?"

"Ran their horses down the way to that barn."

"Without checkin' their saddlebags. If you had you wouldn'ta found any o' the loot. Because they took it with 'em up to the room. *An' left it there*. They left before we did, goin' out the front way, stole our horses an' that fella's gelding, blew the bank, an' ran."

"I don't know. About leaving the loot, I mean."

"Figger it out, it wasn't back in the house in the valley. Oh, it was at one time, but they come back an' got it. Why else come back at all? Bass musta been carryin' it. At least the lion's share. Or could be him an' Collins had already rough divvied it up. But the guy or guys in charge always carry the loot, you know that. Tubal did when him an' his bunch held up the stage."

"I'm not arguing that."

"It comes down to that room overlookin' the street. That's where they left it. Left it to go out an' start earnin' a new batch."

"You think it's still there?"

"If those two whores are, it is. If it isn't, they got to

know where it is." Doc was staring at him. "What are you lookin' at?"

"You're a brilliant man, Rade, you know that? An uncut diamond. Diamond in the rough."

"Horseshit! It's nothin' but common sense."

"I mean it. What you're saying is something of an example of Occam's razor." Raider stared mystified. "William of Occam was a fourteenth-century intellectual, a metaphysician, among other things. A precursor of Martin Luther in his theological skepticism. *Essentia non sunt multiplicanda praeter necessitatem.*" Raider's seizure of mystification deepened perceptibly. "It's a principle, Rade. Simply stated it means that assumptions put forward to explain a phenomenon should be kept to a minimum."

"Somethin' cracked in your head or somethin'?"

"Don't you see? It applies here. The whereabouts of the loot is a phenomenon. There can only be so many assumptions as to where they stashed it. I'm talking logical explanations. Theoretically, it could be back at the house. Moved from the hole under the corner floorboards that you discovered, and left behind when we chased them out.

"If that's so why should they run into Palo Pinto? Why bother? They didn't hang aroun' long enough to get laid."

"Exactly, why bother to stop at all? I can't believe it was to throw us off the track. I agree with you. When they left the valley they took the loot along. You're remarkable, Rade."

"Horseshit."

"I mean it sincerely. I take my hat off to you. You're blushing."

"Bullshit!"

"Horseshit, bullshit, you are."

"If you want to take your hat off, take it off to Bass. It's all his idea. Like this dumb map. He give every man one, figgerin' sooner or later we'd catch up with one or another, collar him, search him, find it."

"It's to deliberately throw us off the track. Keep us running around in circles. *Which we would be doing if we kept chasing them*. Instead we go get the loot. Occam's razor."

Raider's brow bunched in bewilderment. "Where the hell does the razor come in?"

"I don't know. I guess it lops off the string of explanations at a certain point. It keeps the number finite."

"What does that mean?"

"It restricts the number. Prevents you going off into weak and illogical assumptions."

"Jesus."

"What?"

"I'm glad I never went to no college. Doesn't all that bullshit crammed in there give you a headache?"

"Of course not."

"Would me." He got up from the bed. He was preparing to tear up the map when he paused, folded it, and restored it to his pocket. "Souvenir. Let's go. Not to Pilot Point."

"Palo Pinto."

CHAPTER SEVENTEEN

They didn't reach Palo Pinto until well past eleven at night, since Doc preferred that they spare the horses and Raider the rigors of a faster ride. His partner imagined that he was seeing a gradual change come over Doc; in fact he was convinced he did, so much so that he mentioned it.

"This thing takin' a turn for the better makes you feel good, don't it?" he said pointedly as they dismounted up the way from the three-story building into which they had followed the outlaws earlier in the week.

"I suppose it does. If you're leading up to what I think you're leading up to it isn't changing my mind."

"The hell it isn't. It's got to."

"Not necessarily; not at all, actually." They set about removing their saddlebags. Doc eyed Raider, his expression critical, disapproving. "You have a fine, analytical mind, Rade, creative, too, but you're not very good at judging people. Not judging me."

"I'm a better judge o' you than you are yourself. You're not gonna quit. You may think you are now, but you're startin' to edge away from it. I can tell."

"You're wrong."

Doc lit an Old Virginia. A piano sent a flurry of notes, a shabbily executed rendition of "The Old Chisholm Trail" out of the door to Slocum's Saloon. A well-whiskeyed soprano shrilled:

161

"Oh, a ten-dollar hoss and a forty-dollar saddle,
And I'm goin' to punchin' Texas cattle.
Come a ti yi yippie, come a ti yi yea,
Come a ti yi yippie, come a ti yi yea."

"We knew this thing was going to wind up one day. The fact that it looks like it's getting ready to in no way changes my original feeling. Rade, it doesn't affect my decision, believe me it doesn't."

"It's startin' to. It will."

"Why do you want it to? What do you need with a yellow partner?"

"I never called you yellow."

Doc laughed thinly. "For a time there you couldn't stop."

"Maybe I was wrong."

"Maybe not. I certainly felt yellow. I did. I feel it now."

"Bullshit."

"I don't think it's necessary for me to convince you."

"You're tryin' to convince your own self to go through with quittin'. When it comes down to it—the time, the place, an' all—you won't. On account you won't be able to."

"Stick to Occam's razor."

They shouldered their saddlebags. Doc glanced across the street at Slocum's Saloon.

"You're not thinkin' about goin' over there lookin' for your friend the sheriff."

"We really should touch bases with him, Rade."

"Fuck him. He didn't want to help before."

"The bank has been robbed since. If that hasn't changed his mind, nothing will. Let's go by the book. The chief'll appreciate it."

"Fuck him, too."

"If you say so."

Raider groused all the way across the street and into the saloon. Down the bar to a corner table. Sheriff Owensby sat grumpily appraising his hand. He did not look up as they approached. He selected a card and was about to discard it, then changed his mind and disposed of three others.

"Goddamn belly-hole straights'll be the livin' death o' me!"

"You want three cards or one?" inquired the dealer, freezing the pack in hand in front of him.

"What the hell did I just throw down?"

He got his cards, swore, folded, and looked up.

"You again."

"Sheriff Owensby. Sorry to interrupt your game, but we'd like a word with you in private," said Doc stonily. "About your bank that was robbed the other night."

To his surprise Owensby obligingly got to his feet. "Deal me out a hand or two. I'll be back. Outside in the yard, ah . . ."

"Weatherbee. This is Operative Raider, my partner."

"Mmmmm."

They stood outside near a collection of garbage cans filled to overflowing with rotten meat and vegetables. So overpowering was the stench that Raider held his nose. Doc disregarded it, as did the sheriff.

"You two know something about the bank? We rode all over creation lookin' for them."

"We know who did it," said Doc airily. "We also know they'll be back."

"Jesus!"

"Dahhg!" snapped Raider, his thumb and forefinger pressing his nose tightly. "Hey, cad we ged the hell oudda here? Breathin' this stig is magin' me sig." Owensby muttered and walked them down the alley. "This is better. Jesus, what a stink!"

"How do you know they're coming back?" the sheriff asked.

"Doc . . ."

"Why do you keep interruptin'?" the sheriff asked heatedly.

"Everything out in the open, Rade." Doc's eyes went back to Owensby. "Fair is fair."

He explained how they knew Bass, Collins, and Tubal would be coming back. Raider listened along with Owensby, getting more and more upset by the minute.

"You say the loot is upstairs in the parlor house? Jesus, let's go see."

"Not what they got from your bank. Only the earlier loot. We think the bank money is on their persons," Doc continued, "along with everything else they've stolen since, including the Cattleman's Bank money in Pilot Point just this morning."

"What do we do?"

"Keep our eye on the place. Around the clock. We'll take the first shift to say, eight o'clock tomorrow morning. You and your men take eight to four and four to midnight."

"Wait a minute. We don't even know what this bunch looks like!"

Doc described each man in detail.

"If you and your men see them arrive and go into the house, as they surely will, come and get us at once. It'll only be a few minutes. We'll let them make their pickup and leave. Follow them, apprehend them."

"Why the hell let 'em leave? I say arrest them right then and there, surprise the bastards."

"No!" exclaimed Doc.

"Like hell. I give the damn orders around here!"

"You don't order us!" boomed Raider.

"You shut up!"

"Who you tellin' to shut up, cow belly!"

"Both of you shut up!" rasped Doc. "Sheriff, if they show up while you or your men are on duty, handle it as you see fit."

"That's mighty white o' you."

"No need to get sarcastic!" interposed Raider.

"Shut up, Rade. If they happen to come while we're on, we'll handle it our way. Fair enough?"

"I don't know." Owensby's face displayed strong doubts. He rubbed his stubble and studied the ground.

"We'll go on guard now," Doc went on.

"When they show, one o' you hightail it down to my office. I sleep there nights since my wife left me. Which is none o' your damn business. You wake me, understand?"

"We will."

They left him, heading down the alley and back out into the street.

"We don't have to wake him nohow!" said Raider irritably.

"Didn't you hear me just get through promising him we would?"

"I don't care what you promised, I didn't! He won't be nothin' but a millpond round our necks."

"Millstone."

"That too!"

"Calm down. Let's go up and watch the place."

They started up the street, Raider two steps behind. He caught up with Doc as they came abreast of the building. They were directly across from it.

"I just thought o' somethin'," said Raider. "What if they've already come an' gone off? We could stand here for a week."

"Good point. It's not probable, but it's certainly possible."

"Occam's razor, right?"

"Not really." He shook his head, his face suddenly masked with concern. "I don't see as we have any choice but to go on up and talk to those two women."

"The whores, right?"

Doc sighed. "They're still women."

"Praise be."

Their saddlebags still slung over their shoulders, they entered the front door. The bouncer recognized them immediately.

"Where's your shotgun, shitkicker?" he asked Raider. "Some old lady take it away from you?"

"I give it to your mother to keep you away from the house, ass face!"

Doc shoved between them. "Stop the nonsense. Sir, we're not here to cause any trouble, just to sample the merchandise." He held up two dollars. The bouncer's sneer softened into the semblance of a smile. He snatched away the money so fast he almost tore it in two.

"Upstairs on the left?" asked Doc. "The end room?" But he had turned away and was walking off. "Upstairs on the left, the end room," repeated Doc.

They stood before the door, Doc's fist upraised. Raider nodded. He knocked.

"Come in."

Both whores were blondes, one very close to platinum, the other with hair the yellow of fresh corn. They started at sight of the Pinkertons.

"You!" shrilled Platinum.

"Us," said Raider sternly, and closed the door behind him.

The room reeked of cheap perfume. The bed was unmade. Dresses and underclothing hung about on bureau knobs, the closet doorknob, one of the two windows overlooking the street.

"What do you want?" snapped Platinum. Yellow backed away into a corner.

"Relax," said Raider. "Nobody's gonna hurt you. We just wanta talk."

Doc nodded. "We've been talking to Sheriff Owensby."

"Doc!"

Doc ignored him. "We told him something he didn't know—that you two ladies were accessories in the bank robbery the other night. You provided concealment for the men who did the job. We know; we were here. You could go to jail for five years for complicity."

"You're crazy," said Platinum. "Who are you, anyway?"

"Federal agents." They started. Doc nodded grimly. Raider ran a hand past his mouth, hiding a grin, fighting it back. "You're in deep trouble," continued Doc. "The only way you can get out of it is to tell the truth and cooperate."

"Play square an' we'll get you off the hook," asserted Raider magnanimously.

Platinum was trying diligently to conceal her fear. "We don't know nothin'."

"You're getting off on the wrong foot," said Doc coldly. "You know Bass and Collins. They came up here just before the robbery and left a sack full of money with you to hold for them."

"They..." began Yellow.

"Shut up!" shot Platinum.

Doc ignored her. "They're coming back for it, and you know when."

"We don't!" burst Yellow. "They didn't say—"

"I said shut up!" snapped Platinum.

"You," said Doc, waggling his finger reprovingly.

For all her bravado she was still frightened, but visibly determined not to volunteer anything; more frightened of Bass and Collins than of them, he decided. Which was not the case with her friend.

He approached Yellow. "Want to tell us all about it?" he asked mildly. "Want to save your skin?"

"Wanta stay outta Rusk?" interrupted Raider. "They don't separate the women from the men there, you know."

Doc sighed. Yellow was becoming extremely upset, balling her hanky tightly, biting her lower lip, trembling, her eyes darting about the room looking for an escape hatch.

"Sam'll cut our throats," she whined.

"Cooperate and he won't get within ten miles of you," said Doc.

"Where's the loot?" asked Raider.

Yellow glanced at Platinum, who spun away from her angrily. Yellow swallowed hard. Her eyes went to the closet door, which was standing ajar. Raider went over and pulled out a canvas-covered steamer trunk, banded with iron and trimmed with steel. Yellow' eyes flashed toward Platinum. Around her neck hung a slender gold chain. Suspended from it was a small key. She glared at her friend, ignoring Doc's outstretched hand. She gave the key to Raider.

In the trunk were four bulging flour sacks.

"These come with us," said Raider.

"Like hell!" said Platinum. "If he comes back and finds them gone he'll beat us to death!"

"He won't," said Doc mildly. "He won't get the chance. We'll be right next door with the door open a crack. We'll see all three of them before they even knock."

"And you see that you don't tip our hand," warned Raider. "You do, an' ...." He slit his throat with his finger.

"Raaade ... Ladies, just do as we ask. Everything'll come out roses."

"How do we know!" snapped Platinum. "Federal agents! I bet. You could be lyin' in your teeth. You could be crooked as them. Rival gang out to steal what they already did."

"What do you say we run you over to the sheriff's office?" suggested Raider. "You talk to him. Or do we bring him over here?"

"Oh, God no! He comes in here for anything but a trick we'll be kicked out in the street!"

Platinum was suddenly more perturbed and frightened than Yellow.

"Who's got the room on the right just outside your door?" asked Doc.

"Abby Cooper," said Yellow. "But she's away. Gone home to Galveston. Her ma's sick with the pee-neumonia."

"Wait a minute, wait a minute." Doc held up both hands. "I've got a better idea, Rade. What about that bouncer downstairs—does he know Bass and Collins?"

Both shook their heads. "We're the onliest ones in the whole place knows 'em," said Yellow. "Since back to Lewisville."

"Denton County again," remarked Raider.

Doc nodded. "Excellent. Forget the room next door; we'll take over this one. It gives us a clear view of the street. You two ladies are going on a short vacation."

"What in hell you talkin' about!" squealed Platinum.

"You heard the man." said Raider. "We're givin' you time off. Don't say you can't use it. You must get sick to death o' lyin' on your damn backs, starin' at the ceil—"

"Rade!" Doc quieted his tone. "We don't want you to get hurt, and even with the best precautions accidents can happen. They can't if you're not around. Do you have

someplace you can go for a day or two, possibly three?"
    They exchanged glances.
    "Pinto House," they chorused.
    "Good, pack up and move in."
    "Now?" asked Platinum.
    "Now."

CHAPTER EIGHTEEN

Raider drew a deep breath, screwing his face up into the expression of one abruptly seized by illness. He sat on a stool draped with purple silk crowned with lace fringe.

"Jesus, I rather smell that garbage back o' the saloon than this," he muttered.

Doc stood at the side of the window, peering down. It was nearing four in the morning. Raider yawned.

"What'd big mouth say when you sprung this on him?" he asked.

"Nothing much in words, but his eyes said he welcomed it. I don't think he's very interested in action. It cuts into his poker time."

"Yellow as a snake."

"Let's not get into that," protested Doc irritably.

"Him, not you."

He got up from the stool and positioned himself on the opposite side of the window. He studied the deserted street briefly, lost interest, and glanced about the room.

"Ain't it downright disgustin' the way whores live? Spendin' their whole friggin' lives in the bedroom, buckin' an' chewin' strange cock. Disgustin'. Sickenin'. They should be 'shamed o' themselves."

"I . . . imagine they are. I think most of them believe deep down that they're punishing themselves for past sins. And so they degrade themselves deliberately."

"Occam's razor, right?"

"No, no, no."

A prolonged silence stretched between them. The muffled sound of activities downstairs was audible. Up the hallway a door slammed.

"She wasn't like that, Doc. She was a lady."

"Mmmmm."

"She talked like a lady, acted like one. I couldn't get to first base with her. She good as slammed the door in my face. I tried real hard, too."

"Raider, please."

"What's the matter?"

"Ssssh, somebody's coming."

"What are you shushin' me for? They can't hear down in the street, for Chrissakes."

"It's just a hay wagon." He eased slowly toward the center of the window, following the wagon with his eyes. "A little late, little early, take your choice, to be bringing hay into town, wouldn't you say?"

Raider held up a skimpy chemise and made a face. "Look at this—it wouldn' cover the quim on a four-year-old. Which is the whole idea, you know, to tease—"

"Drop it, I'm not interested."

"I was just tryin' to make pleasant conversation."

Rising from his stool, he went to the bed and flopped down onto it. In ten seconds he was asleep, snoring loudly. Doc stared at him smiling, shaking his head.

For the next two days Sheriff Owensby and his men took the day shifts, watching the house front and rear, while Raider and Doc continued their vigil in the room from midnight to eight in the morning. Shortly before midnight of the third day they ascended the back stairs, made their way down the hall, and entered the front room. Raider brought along a loaf of bread and a fat club of salami. Ripping the bread in half, he inserted the meat, bit off a generous chunk, and began chewing. He offered the sandwich to Doc, who politely declined.

Raider ate the entire sandwich in less than three minutes.

"It's no wonder you have stomach trouble, the things you put down there."

"Tasted great." He slammed his belly with both hands. "I'm set now till egg an' bacon time."

"No salt, no pepper, butter, mustard, nothing. It'll sit down the bottom of your stomach like a sad iron, undigested, undigestable. And talk back to you for the next twenty hours."

"Keep me company. It was delicious."

They sat around talking for the next two and a half hours, mostly about Doc's future plans. He had little interest in discussing them, but Raider had the bit in his teeth and refused to let go.

"I been thinkin', you know."

"I keep telling you it's dangerous, Rade, putting too heavy a strain on minimal intelligence."

"You said I was brilliant, remember? Anyways, this is what I figger. You may quit, you may go back east even, but you'll be back. The quiet life ain't for you, Doc, you gotta have action like a hog gotta have swill."

Doc stood at the window looking out. He drew in his breath sharply. "Here they come, all three!"

Raider jumped up from his stool. "It's them, all right, no mistakin' that rooster. Look at that strut. Where are their horses, I wonder?"

"Where they can get them in a hurry." Doc beamed. "At last, and what a relief. I was worried they might bring their whole crew with them."

"Why? It's their loot. The new ones got no claim to it." He smirked. "Their loot, an' safe an' sound with Owensby. Are they in for a surprise. They're 'bout to get themselves a shave with Occam's razor, right?"

"Here they come."

"Look at ol' Tubal lookin' up an' down. Gettin' jumpy in his ol' age. Hey, how 'bout I hide in the closet, make 'em think there's jus' you."

"No. We'll stand on either side of the door. With luck we can take them without a shot. Oh oh, look, they're changing their minds. They're not coming in the front way."

"Front or back makes no difference."

Guns out and cocked, they stood on either side of the door. And waited. The sound of approaching steps emerged from the unabating muffled noise of activities upstairs and down. The steps stopped. A knock rattled the door. Doc nodded. Gripping the knob, Raider jerked open the door.

There stood Yellow and Platinum. And rushing up behind them the three outlaws. Raider swore and pushed Platinum bodily into Bass. Collins pushed Yellow into him. Suddenly all three were in a pile on the floor, the women screaming. The three outlaws fled, careening down the front stairs. Raider battled to untangle himself, cursing eloquently. Doc leaped over the pile and got off a single shot, catching Tubal squarely between the shoulders. Bass and Collins got around the corner. The bouncer appeared, coming up the stairs two at a time, climbing nimbly over Tubal's prostrate body.

The entire floor erupted in an ear-splitting furor. Screaming, bellowing, doors slamming, Raider cursing, the bouncer carrying on like a madman, Yellow screaming hysterically. By the time Doc got by the bouncer, over Tubal, and down to the front door Bass and Collins had gotten away.

CHAPTER NINETEEN

Bass and Collins took the north road out of town. Doc, having extricated himself from the obstacle course on the stairs, made it to his horse in seconds. He was no more than two hundred yards behind the two and beginning to close the gap when, turning and looking behind him, he spied Raider. He didn't slow for him, and it was nearly ten minutes, he estimated, before Raider caught up.

In all the considerable time that had elapsed since he had opened the bedroom door, Raider's anger and frustration had not lessened in the slightest.

"Goddamn stupid bitch-whores! What the hell—"

"Oh, shut up! They didn't do it on purpose."

"Hell no, they was invited. You're the one told 'em three days. As much as asked 'em to come sashayin' back. What timin'. Goddamn son of a bitch Sam an' Bertha!"

"Calm down, we'll catch them."

"We've said that before. If we're gonna it better be before they get back to their place. They make it an' you an' me'll find ourselves outgunned eight to one. Jesus Christ, this kills me! Rips me up an' down! We had 'em cold. Close 'nough to reach out an' touch. Only with them two in between, an' that stupid bouncer, an' those stairs you can't hardly get up an' down normal with nobody blockin' the way, they're so damn narrow. Ever see such rotten timin' in your whole life?"

Doc dismissed his jeremiad with a deliberately theatrical wave. The moon and stars illuminated the road just enough to enable them to make out Bass and Collins's dust. Less than a hundred yards now separated them. Suddenly the pursued deserted the road, pushing through the high grass, slowing their progress, but losing the telltale dust cloud that marked their flight. Raider got off two shots. One of the outlaws, neither he nor Doc could see which, fired back. His accuracy was astounding: The bullet plowed through Doc's derby almost exactly where the first shot had hit, coming up from the house in the shoot-out in the valley.

"My God," he murmured, visibly shaken. "Ewart Bonds was right. He said Collins could shoot with the best."

"Ride yourself lower. That was just to discourage you; the next one's for real."

Raider laughed and emptied his gun after them. Reaching behind him, he began fussing with the twelve-gauge tied to his cantle. Then changed his mind, announcing that he'd better save it for the "close work" upcoming.

They chased for an hour under the disinterested eye of the moon, all but running their mounts into the ground. Bass and Collins reached and abandoned road after road, riding all over the landscape in an effort to shake them. Unable to, they headed northeast, toward Denton County. They crossed the county line and promptly lost themselves in a sprawling grove of trees. Raider and Doc followed them in, warily, slowing, suspecting a possible ambush. But Bass and Collins had no such thought. Galloping out of the trees, they swung sharply right, heading straight as fence wire for a ramshackle farmhouse situated on the edge of an immense cornfield. Smoke curled from the chimney; light poured from the windows. Raider counted six horses in a corral alongside the house, but beyond stood a barn where more horses could easily be stabled. Doc agreed with this assessment. They reined up in the trees and watched Bass and Collins ride up to the house, dismount, and run inside.

"There's your big bay and my little grulla," said Raider. "We let the bastards get settled inside, maybe doze off, an' I'll sneak over an' get those two."

"They know we're out here; there'll be somebody watching."

"When I've got our horses I'll sneak over to that pen an' scatter theirs."

Doc eyed him with a look that accused him of not using all his faculties. "You want to bell the cat..."

"I didn't say nothin' 'bout cats, I'm talkin' chase away their mounts."

Doc admitted to being too tired to argue the strategy. Raider fetched their own horses, bringing them back to the safety of the trees, then sneaked off to check the barn. He came back to report that it was empty. With Tubal out of the game it was now eight against two. Freeing the horses in the corral was, in Doc's opinion, risky. There was no way of knowing how many were stallions; even one would be certain to whinny. Merely opening the gate could easily draw someone's attention from inside the house. In addition there was no way the two of them could cover both the front and back doors and at the same time release the horses. Doc selected the front door.

"It's closest to the corral gate. Good luck."

"Cover me best you can."

Raider crept up to the corral gate on hands and knees, his Peacemaker in hand and cocked. Holding his breath, he rose upward, undid the latch, and eased the gate open. The horses closest to it stood stock still and stared at him.

"Move, you dumb bastards!"

Even as he whispered the words, a thought crossed his mind. He spun around and fled, heading straight back to where Doc lay with the twelve-gauge fixed squarely on the door. Raider was seen. Halfway to safety behind one of the largest of the trees at the edge of the grove, someone inside noticed him and got off a flurry of shots. Cursing, he outran them, diving behind a tree, coming down on his gun hand. His gun went off, chipping bark from Doc's tree less than three inches above the crown of his derby.

"Good God!"

"I didn't mean it! Shoot for Chrissakes!"

"At what, nobody's come out."

None of the outlaws, but the gunfire had set off the horses. Out the open gate they streamed, bringing two men to the door, running out, yelling, cursing, ducking as Doc opened fire. Neither made it back. He got the nearest one in the face with his first shot. Raider got the other with two quick shots in the chest, sending him sprawling backward, banging against the door which had been slammed shut the instant Doc fired.

"Beautiful!" yelled Raider. "Two down, six to go."

"And no horses." Doc got up and, setting the twelve-gauge across his lap, leaned back against the tree. "Let's take turns sleeping. Wake me in an hour."

"You wake me. I need it more'n you. I'm still hurtin', you know, still weak."

"You're fit as a fiddle."

"Like hell. My shoulder's wrecked permanent, aches to beat the band. My ribs are still hairlined fractured. I got a bellyache somethin' fierce from that meat sandwich. I didn't sleep worth a damn this afternoon. I can't sleep nohow in daylight. I—"

"All right, all right, all right."

"That's my partner."

He grinned, closed his eyes, and began snoring. Doc threw a look at the house. The outlaws seemingly had no intention of chasing after their horses, not with a shotgun right outside the door. The two dead men lay where they had fallen. There was no sign of the horses. The wind came up, barreling through the cornfield, setting the fat green leaves clattering like rain on a tin roof. He yawned. His eyelids were heavy; he would have to concentrate and consciously fight off sleep. He got up and got his canteen, sipped a little of the tepid water, and dashed a couple of handfuls against his face. He checked his watch. Just past four o'clock. Raider slept on.

CHAPTER TWENTY

Dawn arrived to spread its flat, white light over the cornfield. Doc had awakened Raider, who sat up, exploring his mouth with his tongue, distastefully tasting his salami sandwich and grumbling in his sprouting beard.

"What's goin' on?"

"How should I know?"

"I think we oughta split up."

"I think one of us should leg it to the nearest town and get some help."

"You already tried that, remember? You know what I think? We oughta slip through these woods, keepin' the house in sight, get round back, an' come at 'em through the cornfield. The way it's laid out we can get practically up to the back door without anybody seein'."

"Then what?"

"Rush the two back windows. Fill the place with thunder. Scare the hell outta them. Maybe knock off two or three."

"Sounds pretty primitive."

"Doc, we gotta take it to 'em; we already waited for them to come to us an' blew it. We gotta get this thing over with. I'm fed up livin' with a damn lit fuse in my hand. Let's go."

Doc was not enthusiastic over the idea but went along with it. Weaving through the trees, they got past the barn, moved forward circling it, and got into the field.

From the rear it appeared as if everyone inside the house was still asleep, but neither was prepared to take it for granted. Each one sneaked up to a window, Raider nodded, Doc nodded, both broke glass and poured in heavy fire, Raider using his six-gun, saving the loaded shotgun for what came next. The noise of the volley died away, and a solitary crow, cawing irritably, rose from the field behind them and flapped off.

There was no sound from within. Doc started to speak.

"Sssssh," cautioned Raider. "Listen."

They heard shuffling, low voices. Suddenly the outlaws came boiling out the front door.

"Let's go!" snapped Raider. Doc reached for the back door. "Are you nuts? You'll get blown in half! Around the corner, an' stick close to the building."

Each swept around a rear corner, making for the front of the house, reloading as they ran, Raider fumbling away a couple of cartridges. Doc beat him to the front and a view of the woods. He got there just in time to see the last of the outlaws vanish into the trees.

"How many do you think?" rasped Raider.

"Probably all the new boys."

"Could be, but I'd hate to bet my hide on it. Okay, I'll stick here, you go cover the back."

"Then what?"

"I'm goin' in—"

"Rade."

"—blastin'. Somebody's sure to run out the back. Right into your sights. Go on, beat it!"

Doc hesitated. Raider glared. Doc withdrew. Returning to the rear, he backed away and hunkered down in amongst the cornstalks. It was all suddenly becoming sloppy, he mused, awkward; each individual step executed almost the instant it was thought up rather than their devising a complete strategy. He smiled thinly. Allan Pinkerton would have been outraged at such sloppy and risky maneuvering. He put a premium on clear-cut planning flawlessly executed. He—

The stalks behind him rustled. He froze. Like a cube of ice, cold steel pressed against the nape of his neck.

"Drop it and get up slowly."

CHAPTER TWENTY-ONE

Sam Bass sat on a rag rug leaning against the end of a bed, bleeding profusely from a chest wound. His normally green eyes looked gray and glazed. He breathed with effort and considerable pain. The tendons in his neck and face were drawn taut. Collins pushed Doc forward with his pistol.

"He's dying all right."

"Shut up," growled Bass, fiercely, determinedly, weakly.

Collins snickered. "He's going to have company. Keep moving: To the front door and open it."

Doc said nothing, but followed each order promptly as it was given him. Outside Raider was pressed against the front of the house, shotgun cocked and ready.

"Drop it, plowboy, or he gets it!" barked Collins.

Raider hesitated. His eyes and Doc's met, and Doc looked away ashamedly. Raider sighed and dropped the twelve-gauge.

"And your six-gun." He did so. "Good boy. Now get 'em up high and get in here."

The three of them stood in the center of the room. Bass groaned and slowly sucked in air.

"Help me, Joel."

"I can't, Sam. Busy. Nobody can help you."

"We're partners."

"Not anymore. It's every man for himself. It's a rough world. Sorry."

180

He sat them side by side in the center of the floor, their hands clasped behind their heads.

"He's dyin'," remarked Raider, his eyes fixed on Bass.

"He knows. He's just in no hurry. You boys aren't yourselves, only none of you've got any control over it, right?" He smirked. "I do."

Collins stood a full head taller than Bass, well and sturdily built, remarkably clean-cut looking, reflected Doc, studying him, for one in his particular line. He looked more the professional gambler than a high-line rider. Again Bass groaned, his head falling forward, his chin striking his breastbone.

"Sam?"

Another groan. Collins went to him, thumbing open his eye. "Look at him hang on, isn't that something? Fight it, Sam, fight like hell." He chuckled.

"Some true-blue friend you are when the goin' gets rocky," observed Raider snidely. "All heart."

"The man's dying, plowboy. You're the one that shot him, Mr. Heart."

Once more Bass groaned. And died, rattling his last deep in his throat.

"Goodbye, Sam."

Bass fell to the floor and lay still. Collins ignored him. He knelt in front of Raider and raised his gun, setting the muzzle squarely against Raider's forehead. Tiny beads of sweat glistened around it.

"You first, big mouth."

"You can't do it," burst out Doc. "You can't shoot him in cold blood."

"Doc . . ."

Collins lowered the gun. "I can't, but you two can. Did. Didn't call us out. No warning. Just blasted away. You're the last son of a bitch to talk 'cold blood,' Mr. Pink. Look at him. That's cold blood. What am I supposed to tell his wife?"

"He's got no wife!" snapped Raider, his eyes narrowing, darting toward Doc.

It was the wrong thing to say. Too late he realized it was

better that he say nothing. It opened the subject for conversation.

"What do you know about his life?" snarled Collins. "Nothing. You bet he's got a wife. Young, pretty, crazy in love with him."

"We don't give a damn, okay?"

"I should know, I stood up for him and Lydia-Mae."

Doc started. Collins nodded. "His best man."

"Lydia-Mae?" asked Doc hollowly. "Lydia-Mae Breed?"

"Don't pay no attention to him, Doc, he's fulla it!"

"The hell I am. That's her name. She's going to fill the bed with tears when she hears. She worships him. But you bastards don't care about that." His face darkened. Again he brought up the gun, pressing it against Raider's forehead. "Goodbye, plowboy."

A gun cracked, so loudly it was as if the entire room exploded. The bullet slammed through Collins's head. He stiffened, his eyes filling with wonderment. For a long moment he remained upright, his hand holding his gun lowering slowly. His grip loosened, and the gun fell to the floor. He slumped over on his right side.

"Jesus!"

Doc examined him. "Clean through and out the other side."

"Who . . . ?"

Doc was on his feet, running to the front door, wrenching it open. A buggy was trundling off at a good clip up the road through the trees, dust climbing from the rear wheels. The hood concealed the driver, but he caught sight of her sleeve as she wielded her whip, the lace cuff at her wrist. An unaccountable impulse prompted him to look down. On the ground lay a woman's handkerchief, white, trimmed with needlepoint. He picked it up. Raider came up beside him.

"Let's get after 'em!"

"Never mind, Rade." He sniffed the handkerchief. His eyes brightened. He held it out to Raider. "Smell it."

He did so. "Perfume."

"Jasmine. The last time I smelled it was coming out of

the Western Union office in Denton. She walked by. I got a second, fainter whiff in the hotel lobby when I followed her in. Mrs. Collins, Rade."

"You're kidding."

Doc held up the handkerchief. "She came from Big Spring not to join him; she came to kill him."

"Why?"

Doc shrugged. "Who knows? Maybe she didn't like his long absences from home. Maybe she heard about the brothel up in Deadwood. Who knows what went on between them?" He stared at Raider. "You knew all along, didn't you?"

"How could I, I never even seen her."

"I'm talking about Lydia-Mae. You knew she and Bass were married."

"That's bullshit, Doc. Collins was just spoutin' off, tryin' to make us both feel guilty for Bass, you know?"

"You knew. That friend of Lydia's, the girl you slept with, knew. She told you."

"She told me nothin'. I didn't ask, she didn't say."

"What are you getting so heated about?"

"I'm not. I just don't like bein' called a liar. I'm tired, I'm hungry. Let's go find the loot, pack them two up, an' get 'em back to Owensby in Palo Pinto. Clean this thing up. You gotta send a wire to A.P., too. Good news for a change. Hey, you look for the loot, I'll rustle us up somethin' to eat, okay?"

"You knew."

"Oh, shut up!"

CHAPTER TWENTY-TWO

They emerged from the Western Union office in Palo Pinto, Raider rereading the congratulatory message from Allan Pinkerton, smirking triumphantly. Until he saw Doc mounting his big bay. He stood watching, shaking his head in disbelief.

"You're crazy, you know that?"

"Please, we've been over and over it."

"We're really not all wrapped up yet, you know. What about the ones that got away from us into the woods?"

"Small potatoes. Nobody cares. We got all the loot back, Chicago's satisfied, the Union Pacific, all the banks. The chief is singing our praises. It's over. I'm free to leave at last."

Raider leered. "I notice you didn't send in no resignation."

"I don't intend to."

"I toldja!"

"I'm going back up to Deadwood."

"What for?"

"I know what you're thinking; she was already married, she was playing me for a fool. I don't see it that way, Rade. We fell in love before I ever told her why I'd come to Deadwood."

"Why do you think she did it?"

"I don't know. Maybe she wanted to get free of him and was desperate, knowing he'd never give her a divorce. Maybe because of the life he lived, she considered him as good as dead already. I don't know what her reason was, I only know she loved me, and you or nobody else can convince me otherwise. She loved me. She would have married me and stuck by me."

"But she already was—"

"Goodbye, Rade. I'll be staying in Deadwood a day or so, then I'm heading for Chicago. To resign in person."

"Bullshit!"

"Whatever you say." He proferred his hand. "Good luck. It's been wonderful. The greatest experience of my life. I mean it sincerely. You're one terrific man, the best partner any man could have. I consider myself lucky. It's been an honor to work with you. Take care of yourself. I'll write you care of Bill Wagner when I get settled back east. Goodbye."

Swinging about, he waved and rode off.

"You're full of it, you know that, Weatherbee? Think you're funny, don'tcha. You're not. That's one o' your biggest troubles—you think you're funny but you never were. You hear me?" Doc waved again without looking back and broke his horse into a trot. "You come back here, Weatherbee, you can't quit on me! Nobody quits on me! Weatherbee! Doc!"

Two elderly, pale, and confused-looking nuns came floating by. They stared at him in alarm.

"He's fulla it, you know that? Look at him! He thinks he can just mount up an' ride outta my life. He can't do this! It's crazy! You don't work a job half your life then just up an' chuck it!" He stopped short, catching himself, swallowing his next words. They gaped at him frightened. "Excuse me, lad...Sisters. I...he...I..."

They lowered their eyes and hurried their step. When he looked back up the street, horse and rider had vanished.

"THE MOST EXCITING WESTERN WRITER SINCE LOUIS L'AMOUR"
—JAKE LOGAN